UNTIL WE MEET AGAIN

A MEN OF THE MISFIT INN PREQUEL NOVELLA

KAIT NOLAN

TAKE THE LEAP PUBLISHING

Dear Reader,

Before I get to my usual warning, I want to make it SUPER DUPER CLEAR that this is a prequel novella. That means it ends on a cliffhanger, not a happily ever after. Because it's backstory to Griff and Sam's novel, *Come A Little Closer,* which is set eight years after this story. **You have been warned!**

This book features characters from the Deep South. As such, it contains a great deal of colorful, colloquial, and occasionally grammatically incorrect language. This is a deliberate choice on my part as an author to most accurately represent the region where I have lived my entire life. This book also contains swearing and pre-marital sex between the lead couple, as those things are part of the realistic lives of characters of this generation, and of many of my readers.

If any of these things are not your cup of tea, please consider that you may not be the right audience for this book. There are scores of other books out there that are written with you in mind. In fact, I've got a list of some of my favorite authors who write on the sweeter side on my website at https://kaitnolan.com/on-the-sweeter-side/

If you choose to stick with me, I hope you enjoy!

Happy reading!

Kait

CHAPTER 1

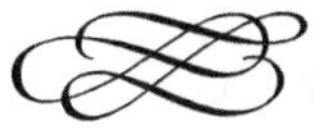

uthor's Note: In case you ignored the letter to readers, a reminder, this is a prequel novella to Come A Little Closer, Men of the Misfit Inn #4 *and will end...not with a happily ever after. That's what the novel is for. Sam and Griff are a second chance romance and this was their origin. You have been warned.*

"BUSINESS OR PLEASURE?"

Griffin Powell cracked an eye to peer at

the petite woman in the seat beside him. With silvery blonde hair that meant she could be anywhere from fifty to seventy, she looked up at him with sharp blue eyes as her fingers deftly worked a pair of knitting needles. Her carryon seemed to have vomited out half a—was that a sweater?—since they'd taken off.

"Ma'am?"

"Are you going to Vegas for business or pleasure?" Her rhinestone-studded velour track suit told him her answer straight off the bat.

"Pleasure." Sin City had seemed like the perfect first stop after being granted true freedom.

"Good place for it." She flashed him a cheeky grin that suggested she had plenty of experience with all the fun Vegas had to offer. "Ever been before?"

"No, ma'am." He hadn't been hardly anywhere that the United States Marine Corps hadn't sent him, and none of those places had been vacation destinations.

"My girlfriends and I go every few years. This will be trip number four for us."

Another older woman leaned across the aisle. "You're forgetting about that trip before the kids were born."

Did that mean their kids? Or their kids' kids?

Griff's pint-sized seatmate considered, then shrugged. "If I was sober more than ten percent of that trip, I'd be surprised."

He gave her a little side eye. It wouldn't take much to send her over the edge. She couldn't weigh more than a buck fifteen soaking wet. "That sounds… eventful."

She trilled a laugh. "Oh, Vegas is the place for that. If you don't come home with stories that can't be shared in mixed company, you didn't do it right. What are you looking for? The shows?"

"The gambling?" her companion asked.

"The women?" offered a third.

Heat suffused his cheeks, making him wish he'd given in to the temptation to let his beard grow in to hide the cursed blush of his Irish heritage. He had a feeling, with these Golden Girls wannabes, he could use it.

"Oh hush, Delia. You're embarrassing the boy," his seatmate told her. "I'm Miss Betty. The shameless one is Miss Delia, and that's Miss Maudie Bell."

Resigned to the fact that he wasn't going to have peace and quiet for the last leg of the flight, he dragged out the manners that had been instilled in him by his foster mother, Joan, before he'd had them further beaten in by the Marine Corps. "Griff. Nice to meet you ladies."

"So which is it you're here for?" Miss Maudie Bell demanded. She'd evidently decided he was far more interesting than the paperback in her lap. He was pretty sure he saw a shirtless dude on the cover.

Oh boy. "Um, actually the food. I'm just out of the Marines, and I've been dreaming about those all-you-can-eat buffets."

Not a lie. Maybe it was sad that his first act of total freedom was related to food, but he didn't have a lot of practice making choices for himself these past four years. The ones he'd made before that had been of the variety that had landed him in a courtroom facing jail or rehabilitation by way of the military. He'd grown the hell up, and now it was time to figure out what he wanted to do with his life. He understood that he had the opportunity for one because of a judge who'd been willing to take a chance on a punk-ass kid, and he didn't intend to waste it.

"Oh, a military man." Miss Delia's gaze skimmed over him, lingering on the ink peeking out from his sleeve.

"We do love a man in uniform," Miss Maudie Bell cooed.

Miss Betty patted his thigh. "Thank you for your service, young man."

Griff offered a noncommittal grunt. He never knew what to say to that sentiment. It made it sound like serving had been some kind of honorable choice. A calling. He'd known men like that and respected the hell out of them. But that wasn't him. He was no hero. He was a reformed hoodlum, who'd learned valuable lessons about responsibility and duty. That didn't make him a good man.

Time for a change of subject.

"Where are you ladies from? I hear some southern in your voices."

"Wishful, Mississippi," Miss Betty announced.

"Born and raised!" Miss Delia added.

"Wishful sounds like something out of a Hallmark movie."

Miss Maudie Bell laughed. "We like to think so. We have a fountain that grants wishes."

He gave the old woman some side eye. "Wishes, huh?" A likely story.

"Hand to God. It's fed from Hope Springs," Miss Betty assured him.

"You're totally making that up."

"No really. It's a thing," Miss Delia insisted. "You have something important you want to wish for, you come throw a coin in that fountain, and it'll come true."

Griff didn't have the first clue what to do with that. What would he even wish for? Not that it mattered. He was hardly going to make a trip all the way to Mississippi on the off-chance this lunacy had a kernel of truth.

"Where are you from, Griff?" Miss Betty asked.

"Tennessee. Little place in the mountains called Eden's Ridge." Not that he'd been home once since he'd shipped out for basic training. Maybe he'd make a trip after Vegas just to check in with Joan. She'd want to see with her own two eyes that he was well and good and in one piece. She'd said so often enough in her letters.

"That up near Gatlinburg?" Miss Maudie Bell asked.

"Further north. Closer to Johnson City. We aren't too far from the North Carolina border."

We. As if it was still home.

Did he want it to be? Griff wasn't sure. Eden's Ridge was part of that past he wasn't quite ready to face yet.

The intercom buzzed. "Passengers, this is your Captain. We're about half an hour out from sunny Las Vegas. At this time, we ask that you store your carryons, return your seats to their upright positions, and fasten your seatbelts for our descent."

Griff helped Miss Betty tuck her knitting bag away and listened with amusement as the three women debated which buffet he should tackle first. By the time they'd landed, he had a list that would get him through his entire stay, along with their recommendations for must-see attractions.

Of course, he helped all three ladies get their carryons out of the overhead bins. It was the polite thing to do. He pretended not to notice Miss Delia ogling his ass or Miss Maudie Bell staring at his abs. The extra sixty pounds of muscle the Marines had added to a frame already well honed by his three years playing wide receiver on his high school football team meant that he got noticed. He was young enough and vain enough to appreciate it, so he flexed a little just to see if any of his admirers would blush.

They did not, but they did ask him for a selfie once they got to the gate. How could he say no to that?

"Vegas on three." Griff held the phone out as they clustered around him, none of them topping his shoulders. "One. Two. Three."

"Vegas!"

He snapped the picture and handed Miss Betty back her phone. "Y'all have a good trip now."

"You, too, sugar!"

"We'll keep our eyes peeled," Miss Maudie Bell told him. "Maybe we'll run into each other again."

Griff grinned. They'd be damned hard to miss. "Maybe so. Bye, ladies."

Still chuckling to himself, he shouldered his bag and went in search of baggage claim.

* * *

"WELCOME TO LAS VEGAS, Nevada. Current local time is 3:39 PM, and the temperature is eighty-eight degrees. As soon as we've docked with the landing bridge, you may retrieve your baggage from the overhead bins. Be advised that items may have shifted during the flight."

Eager to escape the confines of the plane,

Samantha Ferguson unlatched the seatbelt and dragged her backpack out from the seat in front of her as the plane rolled to a stop. All around her, passengers leapt from their seats and popped open the overhead compartments.

The girl with the purple braids who'd been her seatmate for the flight from Raleigh simply stretched and crossed her black-booted feet. "We might as well stay put. It'll take a while before the front of the plane finishes disembarking."

"Fair point. The rest of the wedding party should have landed by now, and I need to check on Eric's flight status." She switched on her phone, waiting impatiently for it to boot up and find a signal.

"You think this trip will be the kick in the pants your relationship needs?" Dahlia asked.

In the way of strangers on a long flight, Sam had confessed her concern about the waning interest on both sides of her year-long relationship. "If it's not, at least I won't be the lone single gal amid all the couples. That would be the worst."

An avalanche of texts hit her phone. She skipped over the multitude of texts from the bride and other bridesmaids, jumping instead to the string from her boyfriend. The preview of the first one had her fumbling to get the text app open.

Eric: **I'm not coming.**

"Not coming? What the hell does he mean he's not coming?"

"Did he miss his flight?" Dahlia asked.

"I don't know. I hope not. This trip has been planned for months." Sam thumbed back a fast reply. **What happened? What's wrong?**

The three dots appeared, indicating he was typing a response. They disappeared and reappeared several more times.

"Come on," she muttered.

The rows ahead of her began to move. She started to rise from her seat, only to sink back down as his reply finally came back.

Eric: **I think we should break up.**

Break up. Break up?

"You have got to be kidding me."

"What did he say?" Her seatmate leaned over, peering at the phone. "Oh no he didn't."

"He can't do this to me. Not now. And sure as hell not like this."

"Damn straight he can't," Dahlia agreed. "Call him."

Riding on temper, Sam dialed his number, unsurprised when the chicken shit didn't actually answer. When his voicemail clicked on, she snarled, "I cannot believe you waited until I was on a plane to Vegas for a *couples* wedding weekend to bring this up and that you *broke up with me with via text.* You are dead to me, Eric. And you'd better pray that I don't send my Navy SEAL brother after you." She hung up with enough violence, she was surprised the screen didn't crack. "Asshat!"

"Your brother's a SEAL?"

"Yep. Currently overseas, but Eric doesn't need to know that." Let him sweat a little over the idea that one of the nation's most elite soldiers had it in for him.

"Seems a paltry punishment for breakup by text."

"You're absolutely right. He deserves much worse. And you know what, I don't even care about the breakup beyond the fact that now I have to tell the bride that we're one short. And on top of that, I get to endure all the looks of pity from the rest of the wedding party, who will assume I'm heartbroken in addition to pissed off."

Dahlia offered her a sympathetic wince as they edged into the aisle. "That does suck. But, hey, it's Vegas. I'm sure you could pick up a plus one somewhere."

"Because asking a perfect stranger to be

my date for a weekend of wedding festivities is a normal thing to do?"

She laughed. "I mean, nobody comes to Vegas for the normal. That's part of the point. To get out of your comfort zone and go a little crazy."

Right. Because crazy was exactly what anybody would expect of strait-laced, straight-A, by-the-book Samantha Ferguson. If she even tried, her friends and family would probably check her in to the nearest facility for a psych eval.

"I'll keep it in mind. It was nice to meet you, Dahlia."

"You, too. And good luck with the wedding."

Sam waved farewell and went to find the nearest bathroom to freshen up a bit.

Maybe Chloe's flight would be late. Or maybe it had gotten here early, and she and the rest of her crew had already headed for the hotel. Sam could cross her fingers and toes that the Universe would somehow buy her some time to figure this out. And maybe somewhere between here and baggage claim she'd be struck by inspiration.

Inspiration did not strike by the time she spotted her mammoth suitcase circling on the carousel. She'd been so busy mentally reviewing the itinerary, she'd missed it on the first pass. Weaving around other travelers, she leaned in to grab the handle and tried to yank. It simply laid over, dragging her a few stumbling steps until she bumped into other waiting passengers.

"Sorry! Sorry!"

A big, muscled arm reached out, snagging the bag off the belt as if it weighed nothing.

Sam relinquished her hold and blew out a relieved breath as she turned to face the Good Samaritan. "Thank you. I—" The words dried up as she took in broad shoulders and muscled arms with tattoos peeking out from the sleeves of his T-shirt. Her gaze traveled up to find a familiar and wholly un-expected smirk.

"Samantha Ferguson." The sound of her name in that gruff baritone had her whole body flushing hot and her brain stuttering to a halt.

Oh my God.

He'd always flustered her. She'd struggled with that burden the entire time she'd tutored him in high school, accepting that she was genetically programmed for his mere presence to make her synapses short circuit. But this… holy wow. The Marines had honed the bad boy athlete she'd crushed on into something truly spectacular. Add that wicked grin and the glint in those piercing blue eyes that had always spelled fun… and trouble… and Sam's mouth began to water.

One ginger brow arched, and she realized she'd been staring. "Griffin Powell." His name was the only thing she could manage. Thank God she didn't squeak or wheeze it.

"So you do remember me."

As if she could forget the guy who'd starred in the majority of her teenage fantasies? "It would be hard not to."

Crap. Did that really just come out of her mouth?

His grin cranked up a few notches.

Yep, she'd totally said that out loud. Awesome. Four years, two bachelors degrees, and a position in one of the top PhD programs in the country, and he still reduced her brain to hormonal mush.

"It's good to see you." Griff opened those burly arms and leaned in.

They were hugging friends? When had they become hugging friends? Sam's inner teen girl hyperventilated as she leaned in to wrap her arms around him. Holy hell he felt good. Big and broad and solid. Her head nestled perfectly against his shoulder as he squeezed her close.

Was it her imagination or did he hold on

a little bit longer than necessary? Maybe he'd been in need of a familiar face. Torn between wanting to put space between them to find some even footing and burrowing in to get a better whiff of that soap and healthy man smell, Sam stayed right where she was. In her world, you didn't ever let go of a hug first. The other person might really need the contact.

With a last squeeze, he stepped back, looking for a moment a little uncertain. "You're the first face from home I've seen in a long, long time."

Sam had the sense there was something a little tender there. She smiled, relieved to see a hint of the vulnerability she'd recognized back in high school. It was the thing that had humanized him enough she could still talk to him. "Well, I'm glad it was a friendly one."

He spun her suitcase around and released the handle, tipping it into her hand. "This thing weighs a ton. Did you bring a body to Vegas?"

"I could certainly fit one in here, but no. More changes of clothes and shoes than I can possibly need. I have to be prepared for anything surrounding the wedding."

Griff went brows up, some of that grin fading. "You're getting married?"

Was he *disappointed* at the idea of that? Dismissing the thought as the most absurd thing to ever cross her mind, she snorted. "Hardly. But my college roommate is. What about you? Why are you in Vegas?"

"Pleasure." Something about the way the word rolled off his tongue had a shiver skating down Sam's spine. "Just finished my four years in the Marines. Came out to have a little fun."

Before she could give in to the urge to ask what kind of fun, she blurted, "Congrats. What's next?"

"An all-I-can-eat buffet is pretty high on the list. After that, the sky's the limit."

"Are you here with friends?" He probably had buddies to go meet.

But Griff shook his head.

This glorious specimen of not-a-total-stranger was here on his own?

Before her brain could jump down that rabbit hole of crazy, someone shouted her name from across the room.

"Sam! Girl! We're here!"

CHAPTER 2

The whirlwind in pink and sequins wanted the world to know she was the bride. The title was spelled out across her boobs, and a tiara with the same perched atop her blonde hair. It listed a little to one side as she bounced over and threw her arms around Sam.

"Oh, it's so good to see you! It's been forever. How was your flight? How was your first year of grad school? I feel like we haven't talked in *months*." The words spilled out in a rush that made Griff wonder if she'd already gotten into the alcohol on her own flight here.

Sam laughed and hugged her back. "Good to see you, too, Chloe."

The entourage—and there was really no other word for the tight cluster of other girls and guys who'd trailed Chloe over here—watched in fond amusement as she continued to jabber. It took Griff about two seconds to conclude this was most of the wedding party, even without the sap in a tuxedo t-shirt staring at the bride's ass.

"—*so* much fun. Everybody should get married in Vegas!" Chloe swung an arm around Sam's shoulders and pivoted, nearly smacking Griff's nose as she flung an expansive hand out, and grinned at him. "And you must be Sam's boyfriend. Welcome to Vegas." In a voice that was probably meant to be a whisper but could totally be heard on the other side of the baggage carousel, she murmured, "Girl, you did *not* tell me he looked like that! Good for you!"

The desire to smirk at the compliment was drowned out by the other thing Chloe had said. Boyfriend. Griff fought the urge to scowl. Of course Sam had a boyfriend. She was smart and gorgeous. So what if he'd had a hot-for-teacher style crush on her during all those tutoring sessions? It wasn't like she'd had cause to give him a single thought in the last four years until the last five minutes.

"Um." Color crept into Sam's cheeks.

Griff waited for her to correct Chloe's assumption, but she didn't. Probably because she couldn't get a word in edgewise.

The groom finally intervened, snagging Chloe around the waist. "Come on, babe. We've gotta hustle if we're gonna make the shuttle to the resort."

"Oh, of course. Silly me." She gave her fiancé a sloppy kiss. "I really love you."

He grinned back. "I really love you, too. Now let's get to the hotel so we have time to check out our room before dinner."

No question there was Thank-God-we're-in-Vegas nookie planned over there.

The groom began steering his bride toward the exit, and Griff couldn't help but notice Sam relaxing at the departure.

"Are you two riding over with us?" Chloe shot back.

Sam lifted her hand in a wave. "No, we're good. Thanks. And I promise I'll see you at dinner."

With an array of blown kisses, the whirlwind got hustled out the door. In her wake, the baggage claim felt downright peaceful.

Sam released a slow breath and grimaced. "Sorry about that. Chloe can be a lot on a good day, and she's definitely gotten into the champagne early."

"No worries. Everybody should be so lucky as to be that excited to get married."

"That is the dream, I suppose."

They lapsed into a silence that felt a helluva lot more awkward than it had before the bride's appearance.

Time to rip the Band-aid off. "Well, I expect you need to go find your actual boyfriend." There. That came out neutral instead of growly, right?

Her mouth twisted in chagrin as she looked up at him. "I don't have one."

That information should not have made him want to do an endzone touchdown boogie.

"No?"

Sam bit her lip, which only served to pull his attention to the smooth pink curve of it. Damn, that mouth. He used to have the hardest time focusing on school when she'd tutored him because of that lush mouth and imagining what it would taste like. Not that he'd ever found out. She was a good girl who absolutely deserved better than the likes of him.

Her shoulders straightened, some kind of resolve coming into her gaze. "Okay, look. This is crazy, and feel free to say no, but my douchcanoe of a now ex-boyfriend bailed on me at the last minute. This whole weekend is meant to be full of couply things. I know we haven't seen each other in forever, and you probably have other things you'd rather do, but… do you wanna be my plus one? They already think you're my boyfriend, and there are sure to be lots of all-you-can-eat buffets, alcohol, and gambling between the wedding stuff. It'd just be through Saturday night." By the end her words were spilling out in as much of a rush as Chloe's.

A good guy would walk away. A good guy would remember that she was still that good girl and deserved better.

But she looked so damned miserable at the idea of facing all that mass coupledom on her own. Griff couldn't blame her for that.

Nobody wanted to be the lone solo act in a group like that. And it wasn't like he already had actual plans here. Wouldn't Vegas be more fun with someone he knew?

"To clarify, are you asking me to be your plus one as myself or as the douchecanoe?"

She winced. "Asking you to be my last-second plus one to a wedding of people you don't know is bad enough. I couldn't possibly expect you to do it while pretending to be someone else."

There was something in her tone that made him wonder if there wasn't a chance in hell anyone would believe he was whoever this idiot was who'd dumped her. Maybe there wasn't. She was smart as hell. Her ex probably was too, his decision to dump her notwithstanding. Griff was just a jarhead who didn't know what he wanted to do with his life. Maybe this was a terrible idea. He was supposed to be curbing that naturally impulsive nature.

Sam shook her head, flags of color creeping back into her cheeks. "It's stupid. I'm sorry I asked. It was good to see you Griffin. Have a good time in Vegas." She turned and fumbled with the handle of her suitcase, trying to escape.

It was the blush that did it. Because he knew her well enough to understand that she wasn't embarrassed of *him*.

Griff reached out to lay a hand over hers on the handle of the monster suitcase. "I'm in."

She went still beneath his touch, and he'd have sworn an electric current shot up his arm from where their hands connected. Slowly, she lifted those big brown eyes to his. "Really?"

"You're the number one reason I graduated high school. Helping you get through this weekend seems like the least I can do."

And maybe it would mean he'd finally get a chance to taste that mouth of hers.

Those lips curved into a relieved smile. "Then let's go find a ride to the hotel."

* * *

SAM HAD COMPLETELY LOST her mind.

Griffin Powell, the guy she'd crushed on for most of high school, the guy who regularly tangled her tongue simply by breathing, the guy who'd grown up to be even finer than he was at eighteen, was staying in her hotel room for the next three days. As her fake boyfriend.

This was, officially, the *worst* idea she'd ever had.

If Griff noticed her panic, he said nothing on the elevator ride up to their floor. Sam used the mirrored walls to surreptitiously watch him standing beside her, with that straight, military bearing, his duffel bag thrown over one shoulder. An air of waiting, of readiness surrounded him. It was a far cry from the restlessness she remembered from all their study sessions. When the doors slid open and a trio of men stepped on, she sensed his posture shift. Two of the men openly checked her out.

"Hey there, sweet cheeks."

Griff slid in front of her and growled. *Growled.* It was an unquestionable threat. A sound of possession. Ridiculous. Unnecessary.

A bolt of heat shot straight to her core.

Yep. Stupendously terrible idea.

Griff didn't even glance at her, just kept that deadly blue gaze on the other men. He'd been a brawler back home. Never without cause and most often in the name of backing up his foster brothers or defending one of his foster sisters. Sam appreciated the idea that he was ready and willing to defend her, but now was not the time or place. She laid her hand on his arm, a silent order to stand down. His muscles were taut beneath her fingers, vibrating and waiting for action, though his hands still hung loose by his sides. At her touch, his head tipped toward her, snaring her with his eyes.

As the elevator car came to a stop again, she found her hand sliding down his arm to link with his, squeezing gently. "This is our floor."

His hand tightened on hers, and he used his bigger bulk to shoulder by the other guys. "'Scuze us."

He didn't let her go as they made their way down the long hall to their room.

"Just curious… are you going to be this overprotective the whole time?"

"That a problem?"

Was it? She hadn't known she had body-guard fantasies before the last five minutes. Maybe it would be fun to indulge in one for the next few days. "No. It's just… unexpected."

Griff glanced down, as if just realizing he

still held her hand. He released her and rubbed at the back of his neck. Color crept up his throat. "There's a lot of fun to be had in Vegas, and a lot of folks who don't know where the line for that ends. As long as you're here with me, I'll keep you safe."

If not for her hand on the door, she might've swooned right at his feet.

But who's going to keep me safe from you?

Sam cleared her throat and opened the door. "I appreciate that."

He followed her inside, bumping into her back as she came to a dead stop at the sight of the lone king-size bed. Right. That was a thing.

Because she didn't want to think about their sleeping arrangements yet, she dragged the monster suitcase across the room and hefted it onto the waiting luggage rack. "We should probably do a crash course in what we've both been up to the last few years so we don't get blindsided at dinner."

"Makes sense. And we may need to do some shopping. I didn't come out here with stuff that's wedding appropriate."

"Whatever you packed will be fine. We'll tell them the airline lost the bag with your suit. Either Chloe will be fine with it, or we'll go rent one for you for the actual wedding."

"And tonight?"

"I've got a dress. Just wear the nicest shirt you brought."

"Got it. So, the rapid-fire catch up. Four years in the Marines. The last two of that was in Okinawa."

Sam's focus lasered in on that hint of ink on his biceps. "Is that where you got the tattoos?"

"Yeah. Most of them, anyway."

He had multiple? She wanted to know how many, of what, and where. But those weren't questions that would likely come up at dinner, so she bit her tongue.

"How long ago did you last talk to any of these people about the idiot ex?" Griff asked.

She had to think about it. "Probably four or five months? They've all been busy with senior year stuff, and I've been up to my eyeballs with grad school. It's easy for time to just slip by."

"Shouldn't you also be in your senior year? You were at UT Knoxville, right?"

"I was. I finished in three years." Easy to do since she'd started as a sophomore.

He huffed a laugh. "Of course you did."

"What's that supposed to mean?"

"Nothing. Just that you're still sucking up knowledge like a sponge. I always admired that about you."

He had? That was news to her.

Before she could comment further, her cell phone rang. Chloe's name flashed on the screen.

"Hey, girl, what's up?"

"Did you and Sexy McSexyson make it to the resort?"

Sam's lips twitched. "We did."

"Great. Everybody's meeting in the lobby in half an hour to head out to dinner. Cody says we've got reservations at some hard-to-get-reservations-for place, so don't be late!"

"We'll be there with bells on. See you soon." Sam hung up to find Griff's mouth pursed with amusement. "What?"

"Chloe and Cody?"

"True story. And they are as nauseatingly cute as that sounds. I need to finish getting ready." She carried her toiletry kit and the dress she planned to wear into the bathroom.

"So grad school where?" Griff's voice sounded from outside.

"UNC Chapel Hill. In English."

They continued their catch up as she did her best to erase all signs of her long day of travel, scrubbing her face clean and starting fresh with her makeup. She put in extra effort because it was Griff's arm she'd be on tonight. Stupid. This whole thing was fake, and her crush was a million years ago. But she'd come so far from that nerdy girl with glasses who'd tutored him, and by damn, she wanted him to notice that.

"One more question," he called.

"Shoot."

"Are you heartbroken over the asshat?"

Sam paused in the process of fastening her earrings. "Not even a little bit."

"Good."

Good? What the hell did *that* mean? Good that she wasn't having to fake being happy? Or good that she wasn't on a rebound because he was actually interested?

Don't get ahead of yourself and read something into this that isn't actually there. He's just doing you a favor.

"Let me throw on my dress, then I'll be ready to go." She shut the door and stripped out of her shorts and t-shirt. The bra had to go, too, to accommodate the dip in the back. A shimmy and a tug and the dress fell into place. Fitted and flirty, in a bold siren red, the 1950s-style halter swing dress hit just past her knees. She'd fallen in love with it on the spot in a little boutique in Raleigh and bought it long before she'd known where she'd wear it. She felt *good* in this dress. Sexy without being trashy. Now she just needed shoes.

Stepping out of the bathroom, she spotted Griff by the expanse of windows, looking delicious in well-fitting jeans and an untucked navy button-down shirt with the sleeves rolled up to expose his muscular forearms.

His eyes swept over her in approval. "Very nice."

Sam ducked her head, hoping he couldn't see the blush as she sat on the bed to strap on her heels. When she'd finished, a broad hand appeared in her field of vision. For a moment she simply stared at it, then up at him.

"If anybody's going to believe that we're together, I'm going to have to touch you."

Well that just sent her brain off on a merry-go-round of lust as she imagined all the inches of skin he could reach in this dress, including the expanse of bare legs under her skirt.

Griff didn't appear affected. He never had. This crush had always been one-sided. Damn it. Cursing her embarrassment, and praying her palm wasn't sweaty, she took his hand, letting him pull her to her feet.

The heels put her eyes right on level with his mouth. That surprisingly sensual mouth she had no doubt could do wicked, wonderful things.

Don't think about kissing him. Don't think about kissing him. Don't think about kissing him.

"Ready?"

"Yes." Oh God, had that sounded as needy as she felt?

With businesslike efficiency, he tucked her arm through his. "Then let's get this show on the road. I'm starving."

CHAPTER 3

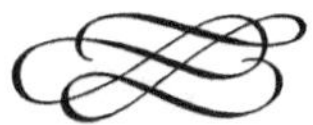

"So are y'all planning on using traditional vows or did you write your own?" Sam asked.

"Writing your own vows is a thing?" Griff thought that seemed like a lot of pressure.

She shrugged. "Sure. Some people have something particular they want to express beyond the classic love, honor, and cherish."

From down the table, one of the other groomsmen frowned. "I thought it was love, honor, and obey."

His girlfriend thumped him on the shoulder. "What century did you crawl out of?"

"The vows might be the only traditional thing about this wedding," Chloe admitted. "I don't have a verbally creative bone in my body. But I do love the idea of writing your own. I bet you'd come up with something utterly gorgeous."

"I don't know about original stuff, but my brain is stuffed chock full of poetry and quotes from people more well-spoken than I am. Kinda goes with the English degree."

"Like what?" Serena asked.

Sam angled her head, her eyes going unfocused in that way Griff knew meant she was mentally walking through that big library in her brain. "I think my favorite quote about love is from Judy Garland, actually. 'For it was not into my ear you whispered, but into my heart. It was not my lips you kissed, but my soul.'"

Chloe collapsed back into her chair, one

hand pressed to her chest. "Guh. That's gorgeous."

Conversation continued around him, but Griff stayed quiet, soaking up the dynamics of the group as Sam's words rolled around in his head. She'd always had a romantic bent. It was one of the many reasons he hadn't ever acted on the attraction he felt. But they weren't in high school anymore.

"Been a while since you and Sam have seen each other, huh?"

Griff didn't quite control his jolt at the question, but he took the time to finish chewing his bite of truly excellent steak to regain his composure and turn his attention to the best man. "Huh?"

Brian shot him a conspiratorial grin. "It's just you keep looking at her like she's dessert."

Well, shit. He'd thought he'd been a little more subtle than that. Couldn't be helped. She was *right there* in that dream of a dress that left her shoulders exposed, with her hair done up in a high ponytail that left her long, lovely neck bare. His fingers itched to trace it and watch goosebumps break out along that soft, soft skin.

Which was so not gonna happen because he was here to do her a favor, not get under her skirt. It'd be great if his dick got the message. He'd been on the verge of popping a woody since she'd walked out of that bathroom.

Shifting a little to relieve the pressure behind his fly, Griff cut another bite of steak. "The long distance thing has been a challenge." They hadn't actually discussed this part of their "relationship," but it seemed a safe enough topic. The women weren't paying attention anyway.

But Chloe apparently had the ears of a bat. She broke off in the middle of her conversation with Serena and Bridget to prop her elbows on the table and drop her chin in both hands, turning those Disney Princess eyes his way. "I've been meaning to ask, Griff. How *did* you and Sam meet?"

No reason to lie about that. "We went to high school together, actually."

"Oh! Were you two a thing back then?"

Griff smiled, remembering all the hours they'd spent together. "We were not. She was my tutor. If not for that, I don't know as she'd have given me the time of day."

"So not true. If not for my tutoring you, you wouldn't have even known my name. He was our star wide receiver. One of the cool kids. We did not run in the same circles." Sam's tone was self-deprecatory.

He didn't like it.

"You were one of the most well-liked members of our class. Nice to everybody. I was just trouble." And he had the sealed juvie record to prove it.

"I was a geek."

"I always thought that was hot."

Sam's head kicked back in surprise as she gave a you've-gotta-be-kidding-me laugh. "You did not."

"Did, too. Still do. All those times you thought I was bored and had to bring me back to task, I was having sexy teacher fantasies about those glasses of yours." Because she looked thunderstruck, he leaned over and draped an arm across the back of her chair, so he was closer to her ear. She wanted a fake boyfriend. Time to make good on that. "You did pack those, right?"

Color bloomed in her cheeks as laughter rippled around the table, but he could see the dilation of her eyes. "Griffin!"

"There it is. That prim teacher voice." He grinned. "Kept me coming back, week after week. I tell you, nobody reads poetry like this woman."

"You hated poetry."

"Not when you read it. Let's see...how did this one go?

'The fountains mingle with the river
And the rivers with the Ocean,
The winds of Heaven mix for ever
With a sweet emotion;
Nothing in the world is single;
All things by a law divine
In one spirit meet and mingle.
Why not I with thine?'"

With every word, Sam's eyes went darker, her lips parting. Griff stayed where he was, arching a brow in challenge to see if she'd finish it. Her gaze stayed on his as she began to speak.

"'See the mountains kiss high Heaven
And the waves clasp one another;
No sister-flower would be forgiven
If it disdained its brother.
And the sunlight clasps the earth
And the moonbeams kiss the sea;
What is all this sweet work worth

If thou kiss not me?"

He wanted to. Wanted to lay his lips over hers right here, right now, as he'd wanted when they'd studied this poem. One of their classmates had totally butchered the reading, and she'd taken over, reciting it with passion and conviction in a smooth voice that was leaps and bounds beyond the awkward recitations they'd been suffering through. She'd read it as it was meant to be read, and the words had lodged in his mind along with the girl herself.

She swallowed. "You remembered."

"It would be hard not to."

Her eyes flared at his replay of her earlier words. It was a dangerous game he was playing, admitting this much of the truth, but he didn't want to walk away.

"Oh my God, you two are the cutest!" Chloe exclaimed. "So if you had a thing for her back then, why didn't you do anything about it?"

"Aside from the fact that her brother, who was one of my teammates, would've cheerfully tried to wipe the floor with me, she deserved better than who I was back then."

Chloe heaved a dramatic sigh, as if that was romantic or some shit. Women were weird.

Sam groaned. "I am totally blaming Jonah for the fact that there was a *five year* gap between my first kiss and my second. He was always sticking his nose in where it didn't belong."

Griff couldn't hold back his curiosity. "When was the first one?"

"Summer camp when I was thirteen."

She hadn't been kissed again until eighteen? Damn. Griff wondered who the lucky bastard was and thought about all the times he could've changed that. What *would* she have done if he'd ever given into the urge to slip those glasses off, slide his fingers into her hair, and taken that mouth? She'd never been immune to him. He'd known that. Would she have pulled away in shock? Kissed him back? Griff had always assumed a girl like her would take a kiss as some kind of a promise. The kind he had no business making. So he'd kept his hands to himself. Still, his curiosity wouldn't leave him alone.

"Who was it?"

"Who was who?"

"Your second kiss." Probably it was some guy from college.

Sam picked up her wine glass. "Why does it matter?"

Feigning the same nonchalance, he picked up his water. "It doesn't. I'm just curious."

"Mason Rowland at the post graduation bonfire."

Griff nearly sprayed the table before he

choked down the sip he'd taken. "*That* little twerp?"

She shrugged, her lips twitching in amusement as she batted those big brown eyes up at him. "I am aware you'd have been better, but you weren't cooperating."

If this is what Sam was like when she flirted, it was probably a damned good thing she hadn't tried it back in high school. Griff didn't think he'd have been able to resist. As the others crowed in amusement, he had to fight the urge to demonstrate his superior kissing skills right the hell now. His hand curled around her nape before he could stop it, and the humor faded from her expression, replaced by something he really wanted to believe was desire.

"I love it when you go all growly," she rasped.

Trouble. He was in so much trouble.

"So how did you reconnect?" Serena

asked. "Or did you keep in touch all this time?"

Remembering they were in a public restaurant with a table full of her friends, Griff eased back. "She had better things to do than keep up with me after graduation." Because he couldn't resist, he ran a light hand down the silky tail of her hair before settling his arm on the back of her chair. Close, but not quite touching. "We ran into each other in Raleigh one weekend when I was on furlough from Camp Lejeune. Talked all night and wandered the city before I had to report back the next day." That was, more or less, what he remembered from the plot of her favorite movie. Minus Vienna and trains and Ethan Hawke. "Been doing the long distance thing ever since."

"That's gotta be so hard." Tasha, one of the other bridesmaids, leaned into her fiancé Cedric's shoulder.

"Definitely not our first choice," Sam

conceded, tipping her head against his arm. "But it means we make the most of the time we've got."

Was there a message in her words about this weekend? Or was this simply Sam playing a part?

It was a question Griff absolutely couldn't get wrong.

THE SUN HAD GONE DOWN by the time their group started back to the hotel. Nerves had kept Sam from eating too much, and the second glass of wine she'd ordered to combat that swoopy, brainless feeling she got every time Griff smiled at her wasn't doing a damned thing to keep her warm.

"It's summer in the middle of the desert. How is it chilly?" Sam rubbed her arms and wished she'd packed a cardigan.

"Easy fix." Griff put his arm around her shoulders, tugging her against his side.

She stumbled a step before he matched his gait to hers. God, he felt good. Warm and solid. She couldn't help burrowing in against his heat. "You're like my own walking, talking furnace."

"I live to serve."

Sam loosed a contented sigh. As they strolled companionably with the others, it was easy to lose herself in the fantasy that this was real. Griff was a damned fine fake boyfriend. She almost actually believed what he'd said at dinner.

Don't be an idiot. He's just playing a role.

"Oh, come on now. We've all got better ways to warm up our women." Cody snagged Chloe around the waist and tipped her back into a dip, cutting off her delighted giggle with a kiss.

That set off a domino effect of the rest of the guys nibbling, kissing, or otherwise canoodling with their women. Lord, they were a horny bunch. There was no question that every single one of them had plans to get naked as soon as they got back to their respective rooms. Lucky them.

As they rode the elevator up, Sam considered it, wondering what Griff would do if she simply unfastened the halter of this dress and let it slide down. Because she didn't know beyond the shadow of a doubt that his response wouldn't be pity or reluctance or any other of a whole host of scenarios that would leave her dying of mortification and without a date for the rest of the festivities, she knew that fantasy was safer to keep in her head. And really, she'd do better not to imagine her bedmate naked.

That was easier said than done, as most of her friends got a head start on the fore-play during the seemingly endless ride up. Sexual tension hung thick in the air, making her aware of every dip and curve of Griff's muscles where she pressed against him. She wanted to peel off that shirt and explore all of them with her hands.

Chloe and Cody were last off the elevator. Cody swung his giggly bride-to-be up into his arms and carted her down the hall.

"We'll see y'all at the pool tomorrow!" she called over his shoulder.

Sam waved back. "Night!" As soon as the doors slid shut, she loosed a breath. "Good lord, I hope they all make it back to their rooms."

"I guarantee they won't be the first to start shedding clothes in the hall if they don't." Griff made no move to step away.

Maybe he was taking his duties as heater seriously. Because she was enjoying it, Sam stayed right where she was, arm around his waist, one finger hooked in his belt loop. That belt loop made her feel unreasonably possessive.

They stayed quiet the rest of the way to

their room. Once inside, he let her go. No one left to perform for.

Welcome back to reality.

To hide her disappointment, Sam moved to the desk and began to remove her earrings. "Well, I don't think anyone doubts that we're together. You've got the whole fake boyfriend routine down cold. All that stuff about having a thing for me in high school really sold it. The poetry in particular was a nice touch." Even if it had melted her panties.

"The easiest lie is the one where you tell the truth as far as possible."

Sam paused, one earring in hand as she stared blindly at the lights of the city beyond the window. "Wait… what?"

"None of that was a lie."

Heart pounding, she pivoted to face him. He stood just inside the room, those breathtaking blue eyes pinned on her. And suddenly it was imperative she get clarification.

"You liked me in high school? Me? Nerdy, bookish, rule-following me?"

He angled his head, looking way too controlled. Damn it, why was he always so self-possessed? "Yeah. Is that so hard to believe?"

"Frankly, yes. Guys didn't like me back then. They were afraid of me and intimidated by the fact that I refused to act less intelligent than I was."

Griff nodded amiably. "Oh, plenty found you intimidating. But that doesn't mean no one liked you. Most were too afraid of antagonizing your brother to do anything about it."

Damn it, Jonah.

"You weren't really afraid of my brother." They'd both been big for their ages.

"No. I was one of the few who could take him."

"Why didn't you?" She shook her head. "I mean, not that I expected you to get into some kind of brawl with Jonah, but why didn't you ever say anything?"

That mouth curved, his eyes crinkling. "Because you, Samantha Ferguson, are a good girl, who had no business getting involved with the likes of me. Trailer trash with a not inconsiderable juvenile record. You deserved so much better."

Temper snapping, she took a step toward him. "Don't talk about yourself like that! That's not who you were, and it's certainly not who you are."

The corner of his mouth twitched. "You always did see the best in people. It's one of your most appealing traits."

He'd liked her. The object of her years-long crush had *liked* her. Maybe still liked her. He'd said yes to this lunatic scheme, hadn't he? And he'd made all these admissions. He'd recited Shelley to flirt with her, for God's sake. Surely, that meant something.

Needing to test the theory, she took another step closer. "So you kept your hands to yourself and left me to the likes of Mason Rowland?"

Those hands curled in on themselves and the look of bemused affection shifted to something sharper. "Not sure I'd have pulled it off if I'd known he was sniffing after you."

Of course, Griff hadn't known. He'd been gone by then, shipped off for basic training.

Feeling a little reckless, Sam inched closer. "I wish you had known. He was pretty terrible." Another step. "I deserved better than that, too."

That coiled tension was back, every inch of his big body ready for action. Every. Inch. It seemed there were a lot of them.

Oh my.

He searched her face. "What are you doing, Samantha?"

Damn, she really loved the sound of her full name in that rumbly voice. "Just wondering what you would have done instead."

His Adam's apple bobbed, his nostrils flaring. "There's what I'd like to think I'd have done and what I probably would have done. You're still that good girl, and I'm not gonna kiss you."

She avoided stomping her foot like a child. Barely. "Why not?"

"Because you are temptation personified in that dress, and I don't know that I can stop. I'm not going to take advantage of you."

Sam blinked. "Oh."

"Yeah. Oh." Griff stepped around her. "I'll sleep on the sofa."

Brain still reeling from the idea that he actually wanted her and was worried about losing control, it took her a few moments to rally. "You're six-two. You won't fit on the sofa. It's a big bed."

"Sharing a bed is a bad idea."

"We'll make a wall of pillows. It'll be fine. Don't break your back on that couch."

After a long, long moment, he grunted, "Fine."

They got ready for bed in a silence that simmered with everything they'd acknowledged but not acted on. He wasn't entirely wrong. She was still a good girl. Still worried about rules and expectations and doing the right thing. How did having a Vegas fling fit into that? She wasn't exactly experienced when it came to sex, but she wasn't prudish either. She liked to think of herself as selective. What was wrong with choosing Griff, so long as it was mutually consensual? And how could she convince him that it was, without feeling as if she was begging?

He was already under the covers, eyes closed, by the time she came out of the bathroom. As she slid beneath the cool sheets, aware of him on the other side of the Great Wall of Pillows, she tried to think what to say to ease the tension between them. Really, what words were going to be a substitute for just giving in? But he'd made his position clear, and she wasn't the kind of confident that could just scale the wall and jump him. Nothing else came to mind before his breath evened out into sleep, and her mind was too full of the past and what ifs.

"Griff?" she whispered. "Are you awake?"

His breathing didn't change.

"For what it's worth, I did wish it had been you back then."

Confession whispered to the dark, she let herself slide into dreams.

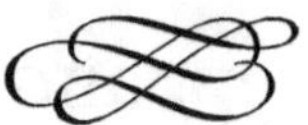

Griff didn't sleep for shit, knowing Sam was a mere armspan away on the other side of that ridiculous wall of pillows, wearing those itty bitty sleep shorts and a tank top that revealed way too much of her breasts. When he finally had dropped off—long after her whispered confession—it had been to dreams of peeling her out of that dress and giving in to every fantasy he'd ever had about her. There'd been a lot of them. He'd woken, hard and aching, to find her sleeping peacefully beside him, one arm draped over the pillow wall to rest on his chest, her hair spilled out like so much silk.

Sweet. Even in her sleep she was so damned sweet.

He'd wanted to roll into that gentle, un-conscious touch. To tug her close and take his mouth on a slow, lingering journey over her skin, waking her with pleasure. Because he had no business even touching sweet, he eased out of bed and carted his ass outside for a run along The Strip. Nearly six miles later, he'd burned off the lust and thought he could face his temporary fake girlfriend. Feeling a little guilty for not leaving a note, he grabbed donuts and coffee on the return trip.

Silence greeted him when he opened the door. "Sam? I brought breakfast."

Was she still sleeping?

He tiptoed inside but the bed and the room were empty. Maybe she'd gone to meet the others for breakfast. Was that on the itinerary? Griff couldn't remember. They hadn't thought to swap contact information yesterday, so he had no way of checking in to ask. Setting the coffee caddy on the desk, he spotted the note tucked into the frame of the mirror.

Hope I didn't run you off. Meeting at the pool at ten for volleyball. Bring your A game! -S

She'd added a post script with her phone number.

So they were just going to carry on as if last night hadn't happened? As if he hadn't admitted to wanting her, and she hadn't said she wished her first kiss—okay second, but did a kiss at thirteen really count?—had been him? Damn it, the run hadn't been enough. Abandoning breakfast, he headed for the bathroom. There was time for a shower and some relief before he was expected at the pool.

By the time he stepped out into the sun again, he was fed, caffeinated, and reasonably sure he wouldn't embarrass himself. Now to find the rest of the wedding party.

The giggles led him over to where the group had commandeered a long row of chaise lounges. Had there ever been a more giggly woman the history of the world than the bride-to-be? Skirting around the changing tent at one end of the pool, he scanned for Sam but didn't find her with the others. Had she bailed? Gone looking for him?

Motion by the stairs at the shallow end drew his attention.

Griff's mouth went dry as the woman in question emerged from the pool, water cascading off her in sheets that seemed designed to highlight every inch of the body exposed by her little black bikini. She was a walking wet dream. And she was headed his way.

"Morning!"

Griff grunted, grateful for the sunglasses hiding his eyes as he took her in from head to toe. Christ, his little academic had a hell of a body.

Except she wasn't his. He needed to re-member that.

"Good run?"

"How did you know I was running?"

"Saw you leave this morning."

He grunted again, his hands itching to touch her and bring all that bare, wet skin in contact with his.

Sam's smile turned mischievous. "See something you like?" The hand she laid on his chest felt like a brand, even through the T-shirt. "I do."

"Is this payback for last night?" he murmured.

"It's an expression of appreciation. C 'mon, Irish, you need sunscreen."

He followed her over to where she was already squirting some into her hand.

"Your back, Marine."

He'd look like a douche if he didn't let her do the honors. Bracing himself for her touch, he tugged the shirt over his head and dropped onto the end of a chaise lounge. There was no missing her hum of approval.

"Very nice."

The sunscreen was cold, but her hands felt so damned good stroking over his shoulders and back, then over all the dips and curves of his arms. A rumble of pleasure snuck out as she circled around to stand between his legs, trailing those hands down his chest. Her breasts were right at eye level, and all he wanted to do was nudge the edge of that bikini top down to taste her nipples. Were they already tight and hard for him?

Get a grip, Powell. You are outside. In public. No thinking about her nipples.

She smelled of chlorine and sun and woman. When he dragged his gaze to her face, he found her smiling.

"You're enjoying this, aren't you?"

She tipped up his sunglasses and gently smoothed sunscreen along his cheeks and his brow, pausing to cradle his face. "Immensely."

So was he.

"Done."

When she started to step back, Griff snagged her around the waist, holding her in place. Just the barest of slides and he'd have the delectable curve of her ass in his hand. "What kind of boyfriend would I be if I didn't return the favor?"

With a noticeably feline smirk, Sam handed over the tube of sunscreen. Turnabout was fair play. Griff took his time, rubbing every exposed inch, paying close attention to each flicker of reaction. The path along her collarbone had her eyes falling to half-mast. The tender spot on the inside of her wrist elicited a shiver and an eruption of goose bumps along her arms. And when he drew his finger along the swell of each breast where they rose above her swimsuit, her breath hitched with a low moan of pleasure, her hand reaching for him as she lifted huge dilated eyes to his.

"If you two are done using sunscreen as foreplay, we have a game to play!" Cody announced.

Right. The game. The wedding. He was not here to talk Samantha out of that teeny bikini. But the scorching look she gave him as she stepped back told him talking was not at all what she had in mind. Griff reached deep, searching for some control.

It was one thing to know that she had a crush on him in high school. There had been plenty of other factors to keep him in line back then. But now, seeing her like this, no longer a girl, but a woman, aware and apparently very willing, he didn't know how he was going to stick to his good intentions of keeping his hands off her.

"THIS IS the least traditional wedding weekend I've ever heard of."

Despite Griff's sotto voce tone, Sam heard him clear enough. She linked her arm through his and surveyed the casino floor. Lights. Music. Opulence. She half expected Danny Ocean to be working his way through the crowd. "Been to a lot of them?"

"No. But even I know gambling isn't a standard substitute for the rehearsal dinner."

The muscles beneath her hand were tense, but not in that trying-to-resist-her way she'd come to recognize. Something about this had him legitimately on edge.

Concerned, she held him back as the others took their chips and headed cheerfully into the fray.

"What's wrong?"

"Nothing." The muscle jumping in his jaw belied the dismissal.

Because she couldn't quite resist, she cupped that jaw, feeling the faint rasp of stubble beneath her fingers as she tipped his head toward hers. "I know you better than that. Talk to me."

His chest rose and fell but he said nothing.

Stubborn man. "Is it the crowd? The noise?" He'd been fine everywhere else so far, but she knew from her brother that all kinds of things could be triggers for military veterans.

Still nothing.

"Griffin." She slid her hand from his jaw down to stroke his nape, wanting to comfort.

He gripped her hip, fingers kneading as

he exhaled a slow breath. "What do you see when you look at this place?"

She considered the question. "Excess… in everything. People who probably want to be someone else for the night. Who want to pretend their lives are more glamorous. People who want to try their hand against Lady Luck."

"I see suckers. Risk." The total condemnation in his tone surprised her.

"I always thought you liked taking risks." He'd been impulsive in high school.

"I did a lot of dumb shit when I was a kid, but I was never reckless."

Sam could think of half a dozen instances where he'd absolutely risked his neck pulling some fool prank with his buddies, but now definitely wasn't the time to bring it up. There was something deeper going on here, so she considered her words carefully.

"I don't think there's anything inherently wrong with risk, so long as you establish the parameters going in. That makes it a calculated risk, not reckless." Did he realize she was talking about more than gambling? She wanted him to take a risk with her. To let him know that they could pursue this pull between them without the strings and expectations he no doubt associated with her as a "good girl".

Griff definitely wasn't focused on the subtext. "Too many people don't make those calculations. The deck is always stacked in the house's favor in a place like this. The booze flows freely to encourage bad decisions. Everything about the design of it is meant to get you to lower your guard and risk it all. Too many people end up betting what they don't have to lose."

He jerked his chin toward the floor. "See that old man in the sweater at the slot machines? He's probably a retiree on a fixed income. Could be he comes in here and gambles away his pension every month. Or that blonde in the silver dress who's apparently on a hot streak down at the roulette table. She'll keep pushing, keep betting, until she takes a step too far and loses it all. And I guaran-damn-tee you there are high-stakes poker games somewhere around here where people are laying down titles and deeds and other collateral they can't possibly afford to lose… because they keep thinking this time will be the time they win."

"Intermittent schedules of reinforcement," Sam murmured. "I remember that from my psych class in college. It's the hardest conditioning to break." She fingered the fine hair at his nape. "Who was it?"

He loosed another of those bone deep sighs, and she could see the retreat in his eyes, though he didn't release her. "My dad. His tastes didn't run so fancy as this. Mostly because he didn't have easy access. But I drove his drunk ass home from North Carolina more times than I could count."

Sam frowned. The Native American casinos were a couple hours over the state line. "I thought you were fifteen when you went into foster care."

"Didn't say it was legal."

Growing up, Burt Powell had been a known alcoholic. It was part of what had led to Griff being put into foster care, part of what was behind his hellion reputation. But she hadn't known this. It added another layer to an already intriguing package.

"You know you're not the only one with a shit father, right?"

Griff's brows drew together. "I thought your dad wasn't in the picture."

"He's not. My mom took Jonah and me and left him years ago. But he's still in Eden's Ridge."

"How did I not know that?"

"Probably because she changed our last name when she divorced him. She wanted to put as much separation between us and The

Right Attitude and its less-than-reputable clientele as possible."

"Wait… are you saying your dad is Lonnie Barker?"

"Yep. The unreasonably proud owner of the dingiest drinking establishment in the county. How he manages to keep the bar solvent is a total mystery. Jonah thinks he's using it as a front for something illegal. Mama does, too. She's never gone after him for back child support because she's too afraid of what it might stir up. And I think she was proud to be able to support us on her own."

Griff shook his head. "I had some run-ins with Lonnie when I went to scrape my dad off the floor at the bar. I can't fathom your mama being with someone like that."

"That's the twenty-four-thousand-dollar question. She says he wasn't always what he is now. He fell in with the wrong crowd in pursuit of what he thought would be easier money than shift work at the factory, and when she gave him the ultimatum of them or us, he chose them." Sam jerked her shoulders. "I don't bring any of this up to diminish whatever your father put you through, and I'm not trying to start a whose-dad-is-worse contest. It just seems like you're telling me this as another attempt to push me away, and I want you to have a little context so maybe you could let me down from this good girl pedestal you have me up on and just look at me as me. Because I'm not judging you on where you came from. I've only ever judged you for you. And I've always liked the guy I saw."

Griff lifted a hand to her cheek, his mouth twisted into a rueful smile tinged with regret. "I'm not a good guy, Samantha."

She tipped her face into the touch, keeping her eyes on his. "Newsflash, Griffin: A bad one wouldn't keep trying to convince me otherwise. A bad one wouldn't have agreed to be my plus one in the first place. You can argue all you want, but I know what I know, and I'm not going to stop working to make you see yourself like I do." She skimmed her hand across his shoulder, down his arm to lace her fingers with his. "We can go. There's plenty more to do in Vegas besides gambling."

He shook his head. "I promised I'd stick with you through all this."

"Seriously, I don't care about getting the casino experience. We can go do something else."

Those blue eyes darkened. "Does that include you inventing new ways to torture me?"

Wanting to lighten the mood, she shot him a grin and purred. "Only if you ask nicely."

They'd definitely crossed a line this morning. The entire day had been full of innuendo and lingering touches. And his stubborn resistance to acting on any of it because he didn't think he was worthy. But she was wearing down his good intentions and didn't intend to stop.

The hand on her hip gave a warning squeeze. "Behave, Samantha."

"Where's the fun in that?"

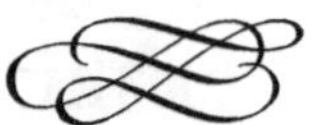

This woman intrigued him. She always had. Griff hadn't expected to be here like this with her. Hadn't ever expected her to want him enough to push back against what he thought was right.

Maybe she didn't come from the kind of background he'd thought, but that still didn't make him good for her.

You can argue all you want, but I know what I know, and I'm not going to stop working to make you see yourself like I do.

What had he ever done to have someone

like her look past the surface? And what would it be like to fall under her spell? To let her try to show him who she thought he was? Could he live up to that expectation?

He could give her pleasure, no question. But was she looking for more than that? She hadn't made noises about this fake relationship becoming real. Hadn't said a word about anything continuing beyond the weekend. If she were anyone else, he'd have already taken her to bed. But Samantha Ferguson was the kind of woman who made a man want to make promises, and Griff had no idea if he could live up to those.

As her eyes shone up at him, full of mischief and clear affection, he also didn't know how much longer he could hold out against her.

"C'mon." Without stopping to exchange any money into chips or tokens, she towed him onto the casino floor.

The murmur of voices, the clink of ice in

glasses, and the repetitive musical burble of the slot machines set his teeth on edge. This was the soundtrack of his nightmares. Because he didn't want to think about his father or the life he'd escaped a long time ago, Griff focused on Sam. The hand in his was small, delicate, but her grip was firm as she cut through the crowd, obviously a woman on a mission. She wasn't here to take in the sights.

They finally found Chloe and the bulk of her entourage gathered around a roulette table.

"Place your bets."

The wedding party stacked chips on various parts of the mat. The wheel began to spin, and the ball dropped. When it came up fourteen red, Chloe cheered. "Oh! I won!"

Cody gave her a smacking kiss. "You're on fire, babe."

Sam slid up to the table beside her. "Congrats."

Chloe beamed. "There you are. Jump into the game! It's fun!"

Sam just shot her an indulgent smile. "I don't think so. This whole casino thing isn't really my scene, so we're gonna go."

Across the table Bridget snorted into her drink.

Her boyfriend Devon lifted his glass in a mocking toast. "Saint Samantha. Always a stick in the mud."

Sam's smile didn't waver, but Griff caught her subtle flinch. This clearly wasn't the first time these people had given her shit. She'd gotten a lot of the same growing up. It pissed him off that anyone was still harassing her merely for being who she was.

He stepped close, sliding a hand around her waist and pulling her back against him. With a pointed look at Devon and Bridget, he pressed a kiss to the silky skin at base of Sam's throat. Her breath hitched, and she dropped her head back against his shoulder, giving him better access. That instant surrender had him going hard, tightening his hold. The subtle scent of—Was that pears?—had him lingering.

Chloe's delighted laugh rang out. "I think Sam's got far better things to do than waste her time in here. You go, girl. Enjoy one-on-one time with your man. We'll see you for the wedding tomorrow."

Sam murmured a breathless, "Yeah, okay. Bye."

He liked the sound of that way too damned much. Time to go. With one last glare at the wedding party, he ushered her toward the exit, keeping her tight to his side.

By the time they'd made it to the lobby, he'd more or less gotten himself under control. Color still rode high in Sam's cheeks. A part of him wanted to continue what he'd started back there, but a bigger part needed to check on her.

"You okay?"

"Of course. Why?" Her voice had lost the breathless tone.

"You didn't have to take the fall for me back there. You could have blamed that all on me. None of them know me. None of them give a shit about me."

She shrugged. "None of them have any problem believing that I'm not okay with casinos. It seemed the most expedient way to get out of here." Her lips quirked, and she glanced up through lowered lashes. "Although I like your way better."

So did he. And if she dragged him toward the elevator and took him back to their room, he wasn't sure he'd be able to say no.

But she didn't.

"C'mon. Let's take a walk."

They fell into the flow of people making their way down The Strip. With every step away from the casino, he relaxed. If she had a destination in mind, she didn't share it. Griff was content to follow, keeping her hand in his while they strolled by the many attractions of the city.

"Can I ask you a question?"

She gave his shoulder a friendly bump with hers. "I've never known you to be hesitant on that front. Shoot."

"Why, exactly, are you friends with these people?"

"I'm not, really. I'm at the fringes, as you might have surmised. Chloe and I are close because we were roommates for two years. She's really a sweetheart, but she's also friends with some people who are… Well, they're not awful people, they're just not really grown up yet and kind of spoiled. A lot of them come from money, from the city. None of which is inherently bad. They're just not really my people. They don't understand someone like me who was in college entirely on scholarship and prioritized my studies over anything else. Who comes from a small town and likes it. Now, I'm in grad school, looking to the future, and they're barely out of school, still just interested in partying." Her shoulders jerked in a shrug, but he knew it bothered her more than she let on.

"You know what I remember most about you growing up?"

"That I was unnecessarily serious? My family always joked that I've been a grownup since I was five. I always caught flack for it."

"You've always known exactly who you are. No artifice. No pretending to be something you're not. Even when who you are isn't exactly like everybody else, you've stayed true to yourself. I've always found that incredibly appealing."

The side eye she shot him made it clear she wasn't buying it. "Really?"

"Yeah. It takes strength and bravery to be yourself and damn what anybody else thinks."

"I don't know how much is strength and bravery, and how much is actually just not seeing the point in being anything else. Pretending to be someone you're not takes way too much effort, and anybody who doesn't like who I actually am isn't someone I need in my life, long-term anyway."

"Must be nice."

"What?"

"Having it all figured out."

Her laughter rolled out. "Oh, if you think I have it all figured out, I'm doing a fantastic job fooling you."

"What do you mean? You're in grad school. You're getting a PhD."

"I mean, yeah, but that's mostly because I don't know what I want to do. I like school, and I'm good at it, so I'm continuing to go to school. I have no idea if I'm going to like being a professor, and there's really not much more you can do with a doctorate in English. But I've got an assistantship that pays my tuition and it gives me a chance to study something I enjoy and have a few more years to figure everything out." She tugged him through a gap in the crowd and up to a railing. "Look, we're just in time."

He realized she'd brought them down to the fountain at the Bellagio. All around them music began to blast from speakers and the lights and jets of the fountain started to dance in time. Sam leaned against the rail, her mouth curved into a delighted smile as she watched.

Griff only half focused on the show, his mind still processing what she'd said. Nothing in his life was even that clear for him. He had no plan yet, not even a temporary one to hold him over until he figured it out. The one thing he knew for certain was that he liked how she made him feel, liked believing that he was more than what he'd been. And maybe, at least for this weekend, he could try seeing things her way.

"Samantha." He rasped her name, and the moment she glanced his way, he surrendered to the need he'd been fighting and lowered his mouth to hers.

* * *

FOR ALL SAM'S flirtation and wishing and hoping Griff would kiss her, she hadn't actually expected the stubborn man to cave. So when his lips touched hers, she jolted and gasped. He stopped in an instant, already starting to retreat.

"Don't you dare." She curled her fingers into his shirt, yanking him back to her.

He needed no further invitation. His fingers speared into her hair, somehow overpowering and gentle all at once. Slow and thorough, she had the sense that he was being careful with her. She didn't want careful. She wasn't fragile. She wanted every bit of this heady, effervescent feeling rushing through her body. As he took her deeper, by slow degrees, she realized that he was trying to give her that kiss she'd wanted, to eradicate every other she'd ever had, until this was the only one she could remember. And it was a hell of an effort.

He consumed her. His touch, his taste, drowned out the crowd and the music and the water behind them. He kissed her until there was nothing and no one left but them. Until he was the only solid thing in her world.

It was the cheering that finally penetrated the internal fireworks.

Griff pulled back, and Sam tried to follow, but she was already on her toes, her arms tight around his shoulders, her body plastered to his, and there was no more leverage unless she climbed him like a tree. She had just enough wherewithal to know there was some reason she shouldn't do that.

He pressed his brow to hers. "Take that, Mason."

She blinked, brain still not processing

anything beyond the fact that Griffin Powell had just kissed the bejeezus out of her and rocked her world. "Who?"

His instant, wicked grin made her want to kiss him again.

Gradually the world filtered back in. People were moving around them and the music had stopped.

Griff laced his hands at the small of her back. "Sorry we missed the show."

"I'll happily miss out on everything Vegas has to offer if we get to do that again." *Preferably with fewer clothes.*

The smug expression probably should've annoyed her, but she was too well-kissed to muster up any irritation.

He huffed a laugh. "Do you want to stick around for the next show?"

No, she wanted to drag him back to their room to do more kissing without an audience. But her brain was busy coming back online, remembering all his protests over the past couple of days. His reluctance wouldn't have changed like the flip of some switch, so full-steam ahead probably wasn't the best idea. They both needed the dubious protection of the public for a while longer.

"Nothing they have to offer is going to top that kiss." It was, perhaps, more honesty than she should admit, but it was the truth. Needing to get them back on some kind of even footing, she let herself drop back to her feet, enjoying the feel of sliding down his muscled torso. "Actually, I'm kinda hungry. Want to go find one of those buffets?"

"I can always eat."

Half an hour later, they settled at a table with multiple desserts between them. Eyeing the different types of pie and cake and ice creams, Sam couldn't keep from licking her lips. "I know having nothing but desserts for dinner should make me feel like an absolute glutton, but I'm having a hard time caring."

"What happens in Vegas stays in Vegas,"

Griff intoned, stabbing a fork into a multi-layer caramel cake and stuffing it into his mouth.

At his groan, her lady bits swooned. She crossed her legs and went after the chocolate pie, figuring it might help soften the blow of the conversation she wanted to have. "So, not that I am by any means complaining, but was that why you finally kissed me?"

His eyes searched her face, the hunger there stealing her breath. "I kissed you because I couldn't take one more minute not knowing how you taste. Because I want to be this version of myself you think is worthy."

She'd known he'd be potent. Known they had chemistry. But she hadn't expected the way his words made her heart stutter. Swallowing against a throat gone suddenly dry, she tightened her grip on the fork and aimed for a casual tone. "For what it's worth, I support this plan whole-heartedly." There was no room to wonder how long this would last. Vegas was all about living in the present, and, right now, he was hers.

He took a contemplative bite of some kind of dessert crepe. "Why do you?"

Sam blinked at him. "I mean, you're a pretty stupendous kisser, so…"

Griff laughed. "No, I mean, why do you have this stubborn belief in me?"

She worked her way through a few bites of coconut cream pie as she considered her answer. "When I look at you, I see potential. I always did." And she hadn't been afraid to defend him to others, even when the odds had been stacked against him. But he didn't know that.

"Don't ever play poker. What's circling around that brain of yours, Samantha?"

She bit her lip, wondering if she should admit the truth. Would it change how he saw her? Break this nascent connection they'd forged? If this destroyed what was growing between them, better it should happen now, before they slid in any deeper. She sucked in a bracing breath. "I need to tell you something."

"Okay." A smile lingered at the edge of his tone, and she knew he had no idea what was coming.

"You going into the Marines was kind of my fault."

"Funny, I remember signing on the dotted line all by myself."

The spoon in her hand trembled slightly. She could do this. She could come clean about what had actually happened. "When you got arrested our senior year, I went to talk to the judge on your behalf."

Griff froze, a forkful of tiramisu halfway to his mouth. "You did what?"

God, she hoped this wasn't a mistake. "It wasn't the silly, juvenile shit you'd gotten in trouble for before. You were eighteen, and there was a weapon in the car. Even though it wasn't yours, they were going to come down on you hard as an adult. It would have ruined your life. So I went to the judge, basically as a character witness. I told him what I knew of you. That you'd fallen into a bad situation with some bad people, but that you were loyal, protective, and smart. I argued that he had two choices—he could send you to jail, where you'd be surrounded by more of those bad people and your path would probably be set, your reputation tainted for the rest of your life. Or he could give you one more chance. That the military would hone those natural gifts into something useful and productive. I promised, if he gave you the choice, you'd make the right one. You just needed someone to believe in you."

Not a shred of humor remained in his expression. The longer they sat there, him saying nothing, the more she regretted opening her mouth.

At last, he shook his head. "I thought it

was just the judge. Or maybe Joan." His brow furrowed. "Why would you do that?"

Because she couldn't help herself, Sam reached out to cover his hand with hers. "Because I knew you were a good guy, even back then. Even under all the wild child behavior and sometimes stupid pranks. You were just running with some of the wrong people, and I didn't want to see you go down a path that might lead you to turn into somebody like my dad."

Griff went quiet again, considering that. His throat worked for a long minute before he finally nodded. "Thank you."

Sam shook her head and started to pull away. "I'm not looking for thanks. I didn't bring all this up to make you feel weird or bad or to bring up bad memories. I just... thought you should know."

His hand turned over, grabbed hers and held on. "I'm saying it anyway. Because my life would have been fucked without you. I owe you more than I can say."

"Don't squander the chance you were given. That's all the thanks I need." Desperate to lighten the mood, she quirked a smile. "And maybe a bite of your apple pie."

After a long moment, he scooped up a healthy bite with vanilla ice cream and held it out. "You drive a hard bargain, Miss Ferguson."

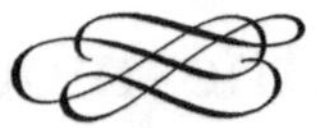

CHAPTER 6

Griff hated suits. Not that he had too much experience in one beyond his dress blues. The one the clerk at the rental place had pushed on him felt overly fancy. Then again, the only one he'd ever owned had come from a mail-order catalog, so he didn't exactly have a well-informed perspective on the matter.

But the moment Sam caught sight of him, he took back every negative thought about it. Her mouth dropped open, and her eyes went dark. She mimed fanning herself as he approached.

"Damn." Her gaze took him in from head to toe. "Just damn."

"You're looking pretty bombshell yourself."

Her long, glossy brown hair had been done up in some intricate half-up, half-down style that showed off shiny chandelier earrings. The makeup made her eyes deep, liquid pools he wanted to fall into. And the dress… Well he'd heard women complain about the hideousness of bridesmaid dresses and thought maybe Chloe deserved a medal of honor and a huge thank you. He didn't know what any of the details were called other than the color—champagne, she'd told him last night—but she looked gorgeous. He pulled her to him for a light kiss he hoped wouldn't ruin her lipstick.

She relaxed at the contact, and only then did he realize she'd been holding herself stiff as a board. Had she been worried about where they stood after last night? Maybe so.

He hadn't taken her to bed. At least not the way she'd been hoping. Despite clear signals she was up for more, he'd kept things PG, citing the fact that she needed to be up early for wedding festivities. But he had relented enough to get rid of the Great Wall of Pillows so they could fall asleep wrapped up together. Well, she'd slept. He'd lain awake thinking long after her breathing had slowed.

Wanting to soothe and needing to touch her, Griff skimmed a hand down her spine. "You're beautiful."

"So are you." She smoothed his lapels. "Very GQ. You might even outshine the groom. Don't tell Cody I said that."

This woman made him smile so easily. "My lips are sealed."

Someone began to clap. "Okay people, everyone is here. Let's take our places, please."

"That's my cue. See you on the other side." Sam rose to her toes and kissed him again. Her eyes searched his face for a moment before she squeezed his arm and disappeared through a door with the wedding planner.

Griff went to find a seat. The little chapel was half-full of guests who'd apparently come in for the wedding itself. He slid into a chair about halfway up the bride's side. Not a moment too soon. Music spilled out of hidden speakers and the bridesmaids processed in, dance-party style. Because of course they did. Sam was second out of the gate. Her face fairly glowed with joy as she be-bopped down the aisle.

Damn, she'd make a beautiful bride.

The idea struck Griff hard enough to steal his breath. He'd never given much consideration to marriage. It was a Someday sort of concept, with a nameless, faceless woman. But as the "Bridal March" began—apparently one of Chloe's few concessions to tradition—it was Sam he imagined walking down the aisle to meet him at the altar. The thought didn't rattle him nearly as much as it should. That in itself was terrifying.

But as the bride and groom recited their vows, he caught Sam's eye and held it, his heart beating thick in his chest.

In a very real way, this woman had saved his life. Not out of an expectation of getting anything in return but because she honestly wanted the best for him. Other than his foster family with Joan, so many of the relationships in his life had been transactional, with balance sheets kept, debts incurred and hoarded, with payback extracted at the highest cost. It was how he'd gotten dragged in as getaway driver for what had turned out to be so much worse than the beer heist he'd been recruited for.

He'd thought about that late into the

night, well after the warm weight of her body relaxed against his.

She'd been gone when he woke, off to do all the girly hair and makeup stuff before the wedding, so he'd had yet more time to think and wonder how he could be the man she'd said he could be. He wanted her to know that he took the charge seriously. And, he realized, that he was serious about her. Life-changing kind of serious.

Was this crazy? Without a doubt.

Did that make it wrong? Not necessarily.

"I now present to you Mr. and Mrs. Cody Lipscomb. You may kiss the bride."

The assembled guests cheered as Cody dipped his bride into a deep kiss. Then they were hot footing it out of the chapel with cries of, "See you after the honeymoon!"

Griff stayed put as the other guests exited. He needed a minute to catch his breath and figure out whether he was going to act on the crazy. He'd been working to control his impulsiveness all these years he'd been in the military. But not every impulse had been bad. A great many had led to some of his very best memories. How could he not let her be one of them?

"Well, that's that. The wedding is done and our duties are officially discharged," Sam announced draping an arm along his shoulders.

He pulled her into his lap, loving how she cuddled into him. "So now what?"

Her expression turned hesitant as she straightened to look into his eyes. "I suppose that's up to you. Your promise was kept. You're free to do whatever you want now."

"I want to enjoy the rest of Vegas with you." *And, you know, maybe the rest of our lives.* But he didn't say that.

"Do you? I wasn't sure after last night."

Hating her uncertainty, he brushed a tendril of hair back from her face. "I'm sorry about that. It had nothing to do with not wanting you. I just needed to think."

She held herself very still, wariness in those beautiful brown eyes. "What conclusion did you come to?"

"That you're the best thing to ever happen to me."

The bloom of surprise and joy on her face made him feel about ten feet tall. "Really?"

"Yeah. You're good for me, Samantha. I don't know yet if I'll be good for you, but I'd like the chance to try."

Her smile turned wicked. "I have no doubt you'll be good."

Well didn't that just send a blast of heat straight through him? "Not what I meant. Although, yes, that's a foregone conclusion." He couldn't walk away from her tonight.

"Naturally."

"I don't remember you having this naughty streak back in high school."

"There's a lot you didn't know about me in high school. But either way, I grew up. And I've got a lot more confidence than I did back then."

"It's sexy as hell."

She leaned forward, brushing the shell of his ear with her lips. "So are you."

"Minx." With a warning squeeze, he slid her off his lap. "We'll get there." That, too, was a foregone conclusion at this point. "But we're going to take in everything Vegas has to offer. Or as much of it as we can cram into the next twenty-four hours."

Sam held out her hand. "Then let's go enjoy the city."

* * *

"Do you want to go back to the hotel to change?"

Sam considered the question. From a purely practical standpoint, that made the most sense. These heels weren't meant for walking, and likely they'd be more comfortable pursuing adventure in street clothes. But given the chemistry sizzling between them, chances were, they wouldn't actually make it back out to see the city. She'd been in a hurry to get to that part of the program, driven by some internal clock, counting down to the end of their time together. But then he'd gone and changed things.

I don't know yet if I'll be good for you, but I'd like the chance to try.

That wasn't the kind of thing you said if you expected things to be over tomorrow. It sounded like he wanted more than the weekend. Like he wanted a shot at a real relationship. A thousand questions jostled in her mind as her need for certainty about that warred with just wanting to enjoy the moment. What was next for him? Would he look for jobs in North Carolina near her? Did he really, truly mean this how it felt?

But she didn't ask. Both because she knew he didn't have it all figured out yet and didn't want to pressure him, and because she was terrified the answer would be no and she'd lose even this limited time with him. Asking about the future beyond tomorrow felt as if it would violate the rules of this place. Like it would break the spell. She wanted the fantasy too much to risk it. So she'd take the discomfort of the shoes and the anticipatory torture of all the extra hours seeing Griff in that suit, dreaming about peeling him out of it. As he'd said, they'd get there. She just had to trust him.

Smoothing her fingers down his lapels, she shook her head. "I think we should roll with the finery and let people make up stories about who we are."

"Stories, huh? Like what?"

"Like, I don't know… an heiress and her bodyguard. Or a couple of actors they figure they must know from something. Or a pair of spies on a mission to infiltrate… well, I don't know. Something."

His lips twitched. "Spies, huh?"

"I mean, it seems like they're always well dressed in movies or books. It could happen. They don't know. The point is, we make this —" She gestured between the two of them. "—look good."

"So we do."

"Besides, you should totally get your money's worth out of that suit rental."

"Fair point. Then let's away, my lady. I have plans for you."

The possibilities had her body flushing hot.

His plans apparently included the High Roller, the world's tallest Ferris wheel. Because he was a prince among men, Griff flagged down a taxi to take them. Or maybe it was because he could kiss her the whole way there. Sam wasn't inclined to complain either way. If the rest of the day was fore-play, the night was going to be fantastic.

At the High Roller, Griff paid the bored looking driver and helped her out of the car, swinging an arm comfortably around her shoulders. She lifted a hand to lace with his fingers, enjoying the connection and the closeness.

"You know, I never imagined you being this kind of affectionate. It doesn't fit with the whole bad boy jock persona you had back in high school."

"It's different being away from every-body's expectations. I can just be myself. And I want to be myself with you."

That he was comfortable enough for that meant a lot to her. Pausing to turn into him, she smiled. "For what it's worth, I like what I see a whole hell of a lot."

"Likewise, Professor."

They were both grinning as he dipped his head toward hers.

"Griff! Yoo-hoo! Griff!"

His head lifted, those sharp eyes searching the crowd. Amusement softened his expression as a trio of older women shuffled their way.

What the hell?

"I told you we'd run into you while you were here!" The one in the lead sported a purple sequin fanny pack and oversized rhinestone sunglasses.

"So you did. It's good to see you again, ladies. Have you had a good trip?"

"Oh my, yes! So many fabulous shows. And Delia here had a fantastic run at the poker tables."

The birdlike woman with the dyed-red hair smirked. "You can always count on those idiots to underestimate an old woman."

Griff chuckled. "Their loss."

"Who's your friend, sonny?" Fanny Pack asked.

His arm tightened possessively around her shoulders. "This is my girlfriend, Samantha. Sam, these were my seatmates on my flight. Miss Betty, Miss Delia, and Miss Maudie Bell."

"Hello, dear!"

"Lovely to meet you."

"Oh, you did good with this one."

It was all Sam could do to hold in the squee as she offered a hello. He'd called her his girlfriend. That made it official, right? The faking it was over. He had no reason to lie to these women.

"What's with the fancy duds?" Miss Delia asked.

"Wedding," Griff explained.

Miss Betty clapped her hands in glee. "Oh, I love a good Vegas wedding. Congratulations!"

"We should document with before ceremony pictures," Miss Maudie Bell insisted.

Sam tried to open her mouth to clarify,

but the women were already spilling out suggestions of the best wedding chapels in the area and instructing them to pose as they held up cell phones. Griff was playing along, though she could feel his body shaking with held in laughter.

When in Vegas...

They took a series of pictures before everyone got in line to buy tickets for the High Roller. The trio of women stuck with them, continuing to offer enthusiastic advice about the best way to get married in Vegas. It was part bickering, part debate, all over-whelming. Sam couldn't help but appreciate their enthusiastic romanticism.

"You two kids have fun!"

"May you have a long and happy life together!"

"Happy honeymooning!"

As the doors to their car finally closed behind them, Sam blew out a breath. "Well that was interesting."

"You did say let people make up stories about us."

"So I did." What did it say that the idea of a Vegas wedding didn't feel as insane now as it would have yesterday? Probably just that Chloe's enthusiasm had rubbed off on her.

Sam moved to the rail, pleased when Griff took up position behind her, caging her in with his body. The wheel began its slow, steady rotation, and all of the city spread out below them. They were quiet, easy in each other's company, and maybe both lost in their own thoughts.

"It feels like being on top of the world." His voice was a low murmur at her ear.

"Makes me want to see the world. Travel is one of those things I've always wanted to do but never had the money for."

"Same. The parts of the world I saw with the Marines weren't exactly tourist destinations."

"Yeah. Mom and I try hard not to think

about where Jonah's being sent with the SEALs. It makes us worry too much about the path he's chosen." And her brother was the last thing she wanted to think about right now. As she took in the silhouette of the Eiffel Tower against the sunset sky, she leaned back against Griff's chest and let herself dream.

"Maybe we can do it now," he murmured.

"See the world after Vegas?"

"That would be amazing. But I was thinking maybe we could do a mini tour right here. They've got Paris covered over there. And several other countries represented in attractions. It might be the only shot we get for a long time. What do you say?"

She spun around, combing her fingers through his hair. "There's no one I'd rather take a world tour with right now than you. Let's do it."

CHAPTER 7

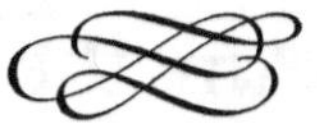

They started with the Paris Las Vegas Hotel and Casino, mugging for pictures at the Arc de Triomphe before heading up to the viewing deck of the Eiffel Tower. Griff soaked up every drop of Sam's delight at the view and toasted with her at the bar in the tower's restaurant. Getting into the spirit, he took her for a culinary tour of Japan, introducing her to some of his favorite delicacies from his time in Okinawa. She was a little wobbly after the saki, so he got another cab to take them to the Venetian.

They'd finish the tour off with Italy and a gondola ride before he'd take her back to the hotel to spend the rest of the night worshiping her body in every way he could imagine.

He'd been imagining a lot.

The boat rocked a bit as they stepped into it.

"Mind your step," the gondolier warned.

Sam collapsed into her seat with a whoosh. "Oh my God, look at that ceiling! Can you believe that's a ceiling and not the sky? It's beautiful."

Griff pulled her against him. "You're beautiful."

Her smile hit him harder than the alcohol. Seeing her light up over this whole experience was so damned gratifying. She'd always given so much to him. More than he felt like he deserved. Tonight felt as if he was giving something back to her.

She snuggled into him as they navigated

away from the docks. Neither of them was paying much attention to the spiel from the gondolier. When they didn't respond, he began to sing, his operatic voice echoing off the high ceiling above the canal. It wasn't Griff's kind of music, but he had to admit, the whole thing added a layer of romance.

Sam sighed in contentment. "I feel like we should commemorate this trip somehow."

"Like with t-shirts or something?"

"It feels way more important than t-shirts. T-shirts don't last. I want to remember this weekend forever."

He wanted the weekend to be the start of forever. Would she want to hang on to what they'd found as much as he did? She'd never been impulsive like him. But the old Sam wouldn't have asked him to be her plus one in the first place. That had to count for something.

She straightened abruptly, eyes going wide. "I have a crazy idea."

He met her gaze, seeing desire and affection and everything he hadn't known was missing in his life. "Me too."

"It's a really big deal."

Heart pounding, he laced his fingers with hers. "Yeah."

"Are we really thinking the same thing?"

"I think we are."

"Okay, we spit it out on three."

Griff nodded. "One."

"Two."

"Three. We should get married." The words simply spilled out at the same moment she said, "We should get tattoos!"

Her jaw dropped. "Wait, what did you say?"

Shit. He was reading this whole situation wrong. They weren't on the same page after all. "Nothing."

Her hand curled around his arm. "You just said we should get married."

Griff studied her face, desperately trying to figure out whether he should pretend to be drunker than he was. He forced a cocky smile. "I mean, you did want something big. I can't think of much bigger than that. But we could do tattoos instead. Do you have any?" He hadn't seen any when she'd been in that teeny bikini, but that didn't rule them out.

She stared at him for a long moment before seeming to dismiss his crazy idea. "No, but I always wanted one. What do you think?"

A permanent mark to signify the permanent impact she'd had on his life? If he didn't get her forever, that would be something. "I'm in. Let's do it."

"If you're looking for a fantastic tattoo artist, go to Desert Ink. Tell them Marco from the Venetian sent you."

Sam shot the gondolier a sweet smile as

they reached the dock again. "Thank you for a wonderful ride and for the rec."

"Sure thing." As Griff handed Sam out of the gondola, the gondolier leaned in and added, "And if you do opt for the wedding, there's a great twenty-four hour place right next door."

Griff held in his wince. "Thanks, man."

They stopped for dessert first. By the time they'd polished off a plateful of Italian wedding cookies, the buzz from their earlier drinks had worn off. Sam didn't bring up his blurted proposal, and Griff couldn't decide whether he was relieved or not. Maybe she wasn't feeling the same thing he was. Maybe this was just a weekend for her. She hadn't asked for more than that, so he really didn't have a right to be disappointed if it ended there. He'd take what she'd give him and be grateful. But he'd felt like they were on the precipice of something bigger.

Because it was within walking distance,

they went to the tattoo shop on foot. As they stood in the glow of the neon sign, Griff tugged her into his arms again. "You still want to do this?"

Her eyes narrowed. "Do you think I'm too much of a good girl for a tattoo?"

"No. I just want to make sure you're sober enough to make the decision to put something permanently on your body and not regret it tomorrow."

"I'm not going to regret anything tomorrow. C'mon. Let's do this."

She dragged him into the shop. A girl with purple braids, a nose ring, and multiple ear piercings sat behind the counter. "Can I help you?" Taking a good look at Sam, she did a double-take. "Well, hi again."

"Dahlia! Hi!"

Purple Braids glanced from her to Griff and back again. "I see you found your plus one."

Sam beamed. "I certainly did. Griff and I

went to high school together. We ran into each other at baggage claim and reconnected."

Dahlia nodded sagely. "So not a stranger after all. Looks like that worked out."

"You have no idea."

Griff arched a brow. "Um… what's happening?"

"Dahlia was my seatmate on the way to Vegas. She was there for the dumping by text. It was her idea that I find another plus one for the wedding."

Griff laid a hand over his heart. "Then let me offer my profound gratitude."

Dahlia grinned. "I love it when a plan comes together. What can I do for you two?"

"We're here to get tattoos. Marco from the Venetian sent us."

"I can help you with that. Do you know what you want?"

Griff looked at Sam. "I have a suggestion."

"Lay it on me."

"We want to commemorate the trip, right?"

She nodded.

"What about that thing you said at dinner the other night? The Judy Garland quote."

Her eyes went shiny. "Griff."

"I mean, speaking for myself, it fits the bill. But we can keep looking. I know that might be a lot." And why the hell was he pushing this? She'd already neatly avoided the subject of his bumbled proposal. Maybe this didn't all mean as much to her as it did to him.

But she reached up to cup his cheek. "It's perfect."

They discussed fonts and placement, and then Dahlia went to work. Because he'd done it before, Griff went first. It felt right, inking these words into his skin over the heart she'd slid into. A link. A piece of truth.

"Looks good." Dahlia smoothed a Saniderm bandage over the fresh tattoo. "Let's get to part two. Sam?"

Griff slid off the table shrugged into his shirt. "You're up, gorgeous." He didn't miss the appreciative gaze Sam raked over him. At the very least, she still wanted him.

"Where are we putting this thing?" Dahlia asked.

"Not sure. It's my first one. What do you suggest?"

"Forearms are good locations for quotes. Above or below the collar bone. Shoulders. Down the torso. Over the ribs."

"Not the forearm. And anywhere near the collar bone seems like it'd be painful. What do you think, Griff?"

Letting his gaze track over her, he imagined the words on her skin, a companion to his. "I think the shoulder. Here. It's less sensitive." Reaching out, he trailed a finger along her skin, just above the back of her dress, where he wanted to trace with his lips.

She shivered at the touch. "I don't know about less sensitive, but I like it."

Ignoring the innuendo, Dahlia nodded. "Shoulder it is. On your stomach."

Sam got into position, and Dahlia edged the zipper down so she could work unencumbered. Griff tried hard not to think about lowering that zipper later and how that champagne dress would look on the floor.

"Will it hurt much?"

"A bit like a sunburn. If it gets to be too much, just let me know and we can pause for a bit." Dahlia cleaned the area with alcohol, then went to retrieve the transfer in the font Sam had chosen.

"Griff?"

He circled around in front of her. "Yeah, Professor?"

"Hold my hand?"

Without hesitation, he snagged a spare stool and rolled it over so he could lace his fingers with hers. "Nervous?"

"A little."

"You absolutely sure? It's your last chance to back out."

Her eyes seemed suddenly very serious. "I don't want to back out."

Were they still talking about tattoos? Or was she thinking about the wedding-white elephant they weren't discussing?

Dahlia returned with the transfer from the printer. "Ready to rock and roll?"

Sam kept her gaze on his. "I'm ready."

As tattoos went, hers didn't take too long. She winced several times but otherwise didn't flinch. Griff squeezed her hand when pain flickered over her face so she'd focused on the pressure instead of the sting on her shoulder. When Dahlia lifted the tattoo gun at last, Sam exhaled a long, slow breath.

"All done, champ." Griff grinned at her. "Want me to take a pic so you can see? It's probably a little easier than twisting around to see in a mirror just now."

"Yeah."

Dahlia leaned back so he could get the shot, then applied the bandage to the fresh ink and zipped up the dress. "You're all set."

Sam sat up and swayed. "I'm a little woozy."

"That'll pass. It's the adrenaline dump. Here, check it out." Griff leaned against the tattoo table to show her the picture.

"Oh, it's beautiful." Her finger traced the image on the phone, a smile curving her lips. "I love it."

"You did good for a first-timer," Dahlia informed her. "Feel free to sit for a bit while I get ready to ring you up."

Sam leaned against him, and mindful of her new tattoo, Griff put an arm around her.

"So where to next?" he asked.

"That thing you said earlier on the gondola—"

Oh shit.

"Was it because you felt like that was a condition of taking me to bed? Because of the good girl thing?"

"What? No. I only need your clear consent for that."

She angled her head to look up at him. "Then why?"

He could explain it away, tell her he hadn't been serious. But that somehow felt like a betrayal. So he swallowed and admitted the truth. "Because I want to. Because I meant what I said earlier, and I don't want to just try for the weekend. I know it's crazy and impulsive, and you're neither of those things. Probably it's a good for one of us to keep our head about all this."

"Yes."

His heart sank, but he kept his smile glued in place. "It's fine. No hard feelings. It was just—"

She turned into him, her hands skimming up his chest. "No. I'm saying yes. To you."

He pinned her hand over his heart, feeling the heat of her touch where it pounded. "Really? Seriously? Are you sure?"

Her smile bloomed like a sunrise. "Let's do it."

* * *

THEY HIT up the chapel next door first, putting down a deposit for the staff to get started setting up the ceremony, while they went across town to apply for a marriage license. Giddiness fizzed in Sam's blood like champagne. If this was a dream, she didn't want to wake up.

The boy she'd crushed on for years had grown into a man she could respect, one she loved. Perhaps she'd always loved Griff, but she'd never imagined he'd love her back. Never imagined he'd want to spend more than the night, the weekend with her. And he wanted a lifetime. He'd inked those feelings into his skin, as she had her own. Then they inked their names on the paperwork, and the whole thing began to feel real.

On the cab ride back to the chapel, she waited for the panic, the doubt, to creep in on little cat feet. But nothing about marrying him felt crazy. It simply felt like the right next step. Saint Samantha was accepting this miracle and taking the leap, knowing her man would catch her. Wouldn't that shock her friends to hell and back?

"The paperwork is all in order. Excellent. You just need to select the rings. We have a lovely selection just over here."

They trailed the slim, classy blonde with Dolly Parton hair over to a jewelry case and peered inside.

Catching Griff's frown, Sam leaned into him. "What is it?"

"I should've gotten you a ring."

"We're about to give each other rings. I don't need something fancy. It's just the symbolism of the thing." She leaned over, pointed to a pair of simple gold bands. "What about those?"

"They're pretty plain."

"Classic," she corrected.

"Okay."

The blonde clasped her hands. "Wonderful. Let's just get your sizes."

As soon as that was decided, Sheryl directed them to what she referred to as "The Little Chapel." The tiny room had only four rows of pews that could seat maybe two or three people each. The walls were swagged in tulle and ribbon, with twinkle lights wrapping up faux columns and a profusion of flowers in large urns at the front by the altar.

A man in a sober gray suit, with a beatific smile and a Bible in his hand, met them at the door. "Before you take your places, would you prefer traditional vows or do you have your own?"

"I have something in mind." Griff raised a brow. "You okay with nontraditional?"

Sam's lips twitched. "Well, I'm here, so… Yeah, nontraditional is fine." She had a riot of words from poets and playwrights and all the literature she loved spiraling through her mind. The right thing would rise to the surface.

"Okay. Griffin, would you take your place at the front, please?" Sheryl gestured with one manicured hand.

He nodded, pausing for a quick kiss across Sam's knuckles that set off sparklers in her blood. "See you up there."

She took her own place at the back of the chapel, accepting the bouquet Sheryl offered. Music began to play, and only then did she feel the pinch around her heart. She'd always imagined having her family around for her wedding. Having Jonah to walk her down the aisle. But she could see Griff waiting for her. Solid, steady, and impossibly hers. She didn't want to wait for another time and place. She wanted this now.

Floating down the short aisle, she barely heard the music. As he took her hands and smiled, she thought her thundering heart would simply burst with the joy of it. The officiant began to speak. Questions were asked and answered. And then she was asked for her vows.

"There are others who've put this better than I could. I hope you don't mind if I reach for their words right now."

Griff squeezed her hands. "I plan the same."

Gaze locked on his face, she spoke the lines that had long ago etched on her heart from *Captain Corelli's Mandolin.* "'Love is a temporary madness, it erupts like volcanoes and then subsides. And when it subsides you have to make a decision. You have to work out whether your roots have so entwined together that it is inconceivable that you should ever part. Because this is what love is. Love is not breathlessness, it is not excitement, it is not the promulgation of eternal passion. That is just being 'in love' which any fool can do. Love itself is what is left over when being in love has burned away, and this is both an art and a fortunate accident. Those that truly love, have roots that grow towards each other underground, and when all the pretty blossoms have fallen from their branches, they find that they are one tree and not two.'

"I pledge to twine my roots, my fate, with yours from this day forward."

The hands she held trembled, and emotion swam into those beautiful blue eyes. His throat worked for a long moment before he began to speak.

"'I love you,

Not only for what you are,
But for what I am
When I am with you.
I love you,
Not only for what
You have made of yourself,
But for what
You are making of me.
I love you
For the part of me
That you bring out;
I love you
For putting your hand
Into my heaped-up heart
And passing over
All the foolish, weak things
That you can't help
Dimly seeing there,
And for drawing out
Into the light
All the beautiful belongings
That no one else had looked

Quite far enough to find.
I love you
Because you have done
More than any creed
Could have done
To make me good,
And more than any fate
To make me happy.'"

He swallowed again. "I pledge to do all that I can to deserve you, though it may take a lifetime."

Sam recognized the poem but was too overcome to remember the author. He loved her. He *loved* her. It didn't matter that it was a quote rather than his own words. His recitation had been full of feeling, his voice unwavering with the promise, and she had to fight against the tears of joy.

"Lovely," the officiant murmured. "And now the exchange of rings."

Sam kept her gaze on Griff's as they repeated the words, slid those circles of gold onto each other's fingers. She soaked up the sound of his contented sigh, the warmth of his hands around hers, committing the moment to memory.

And then it was done.

"By the power vested in me by the state of Nevada, I now pronounce you husband and wife. You may kiss the bride."

Griff reeled her in, and she could taste his smile as he laid his lips over hers in their first, official, married kiss.

Twining her arms around his shoulders, she couldn't wait for the rest.

* * *

MARRYING a Marine absolutely had its perks. Sam's new husband—*husband*, holy shit!—carried her down the hall and over the threshold to their room as if she weighed no more than a kitten. Her romantic heart swooned and began to pound as he booted the door shut with his foot. At long last they'd finally get to give in to all this heat that had been building between them.

Beyond tired of waiting, she rained kissed over his face, down his throat. "I can't wait to get naked with you. I want to feel your hands everywhere."

Those hands tightened around her as he groaned. "We'll get there. But we're gonna take our time about it."

Sam pulled back, fully prepared to campaign for why they should shoot for fast first and slow later. Then she caught sight of the room. Rose petals had been scattered over the bed and floor. Electric candles glimmered on almost every horizontal surface. Champagne chilled in a silver bucket beside a tray of chocolate-covered strawberries. Her heart melted. "Oh! When did… how did you do this?"

"I had the chapel call the hotel to set it up. I wanted tonight to be special for you."

She framed his face, loving the way his eyes darkened. "Everything about this weekend has been special."

Wanting to thank him and lacking the words, she laid her lips over his again, hoping he could taste the depth of her feeling. He shifted, gently lowering her body and drawing her in to take the kiss deeper. Her muscles loosened, heat pooling low in her belly as she willingly sank into the drugging haze of arousal. She expected him to back her toward the bed, to start undressing her.

Instead, he stopped, skimming his fingers through her hair. "I want to toast."

"Okay." Her voice was breathless with wanting. But she could wait. They had time. A lifetime.

Griff stepped away, twisting open the champagne. They both grinned at the celebratory pop of the cork. He tipped the fizzy golden liquid into waiting flutes and passed her one before lifting his own.

"To your idiot ex."

Sam grimaced. "I don't really want to think about him in this moment."

"Bear with me. Without him we might never have reconnected, never have found this."

She angled her head in concession. "Okay, fair point. To Eric the Idiot for exiting my life at the best possible moment."

They clinked glasses and drank. The bubbles burst against her tongue. More fizzed in her blood at the look in Griff's eyes as he continued.

"To us and this big, brand new adventure."

Again they toasted, the ring of tapping glasses another entry to their soundtrack of the night.

His lips curved. "To you, for being you.

Brilliant and beautiful and exactly what I need."

It was a joy and a blessing to be appreciated for who and what she was, exactly as she was. Wanting him to feel the same, Sam raised her glass again. "To risk and incalculable reward. I always knew you'd turn out to be an amazing man. I just never expected you to be mine."

He hesitated a beat before draining the rest of his glass. She knew he'd never been easy with praise. She'd have to work on that. But right now, she wanted her husband, and it was time to get this show on the road.

Finishing her champagne, she snagged his glass and set them both aside before taking matters into her own hands. It took mere seconds to drag down her zipper. With a few delicate shrugs, she let the dress fall to the floor in a pool of fabric, leaving her standing in nothing but a thong. Whatever nerves she might've had about him seeing her all but naked were quickly extinguished by the instant flare of hunger in his eyes.

Swallowing, she lifted her chin with what she hoped was a come-hither stare. "Now, come and claim your wife."

With a delicious growl, he boosted her up so she could wrap her legs around his waist. The bulge of his erection pressed against her center as he took her mouth in a hungry kiss that seemed to go from zero to sixty in less than a second. They tumbled onto the bed and the weight of him was glorious. Her hands shoved at his coat, and he reared back, tossing it to the side and dragging his shirt over his head in one smooth move that left his chest bare.

The companion tattoo to hers stood out stark against his chest. But Sam had only a moment to take it in before he came back to her, taking his lips on a sprinting journey down her throat and chest to lay claim to her breasts. As his tongue curled around one nipple, she bowed up, sensation shooting through her body like lightning.

"Oh God, please." She didn't know exactly what she was begging for. More? Less?

But he knew better than she. His hand skated down her torso, over her belly to slip between her legs, cupping the heat there with his big, broad palm.

She arched into the touch. "Griff! More. Please."

"So polite," he rumbled.

The self-satisfied smirk should maybe be annoying but she was too close to the edge to complain. Switching to her other breast, he sucked her nipple, caressing it with his tongue as he rubbed the heel of his hand against her mound. She lifted her hips against him, seeking more pressure, fisting her hand in his hair.

"Oh God, I'm so… I'm going to…"

"Come for me, sweet girl." As he gave the order, he nudged aside the soaked fabric of her underwear and drew his finger through her folds.

She shattered, her whole body convulsing.

He kissed her again, and she could taste his smile as he eased her back down. When she went limp, he pulled back, kissing his way down her body, taking the panties as he went.

A moment, a heartbeat, a year later he came back, nudging her thighs apart and pressing a kiss to her knee before settling between them. Sam trembled. "What are you…"

But his intent was obvious as he stared up at her with hooded eyes.

"I don't… I can't possibly."

Griff stroked her leg. "Oh, you most definitely can."

Swallowing hard, she squeezed her eyes shut. "Um. No one's ever done… that."

He made some sound low in his throat,

primitive, primal. Possessive. "I love that I'll be your first. And your last."

Before she had a moment to wrap her mind around that, his mouth was on her and she lost whatever last grasp of words she'd had left. She whimpered and writhed, gasping his name as he licked and sucked and drove her mad. It was too much and not enough. Pressure built and built but she couldn't quite get there again. Then he slid one thick finger into her and curled.

She shot over the edge into a total freefall, blind and deaf and utterly out of control. But Griff was there. Holding her. Kissing her. Grounding her.

He stroked the hair back from her face. "Samantha."

She shuddered at the sound of her name in this devastatingly intimate voice. Or maybe that was more aftershocks. "Griffin." His name came out barely above a whisper.

"There's something we need to discuss."

Discuss? Was he kidding? That would require those things… What were they called? Words? She must've made some incredulous sound because he huffed a laugh, pressing a kiss to her shoulder.

"Is this your first time? Not just that, but the rest of this."

Sam blinked at him for a moment, absorbing his serious expression before she finally realized what he was asking. "No." There'd only been two before and neither of them had managed what he had with only his mouth and hands.

"Okay. I think you're ready." Suddenly the room was shifting as he rolled them so she straddled his hips. "You should have control here."

Somewhere along the way, he'd stripped out of the rest of his clothes and donned a condom. Sam glanced down to take in the erection pressed between them. "Wow. You're… wow."

"Might be a bit tight. Take your time."

Curling her hand around him, she gave an experimental stroke, loving the way he jumped in her palm.

"Professor, if you don't want this over before it starts, you'll want to stop that. You can play later."

Chuckling, she bent to kiss him again, nipping at his bottom lip. "You can be sure that I will." She wanted to explore him, learn all of his intimate secrets as he was learning hers.

"Promises promises."

Sobering, she rose up and positioned him at her entrance. "I've wanted you for a very, very long time."

"Likewise."

Linking her hands with his, Sam held his gaze as she began the long, slow slide down. Even with all his ministrations, he was big, and they were a snug fit. Her thighs worked as she rose and fell, taking him incrementally deeper. Griff held himself still, and she could feel the shudder in his muscles from the effort to let her set the pace.

He brought their joined hands to his lips. "Breathe, baby."

Her breath sighed out, only to catch again as he filled her completely.

"Okay?"

"Yeah," she whispered, her throat going as tight as her body around him. "I just… This is… You're…" *Everything.*

But she didn't know how to say it. Even now, with absolutely no barriers left between them, she couldn't bring herself to admit the truth. That she loved him. That she'd loved him for years.

Her gaze zeroed in on the twin gold bands on their twined fingers. Giving up on speech, she bent forward, pressing her own lips to those rings. Their new beginning.

The position shifted him inside her, and he groaned, thrusting his hips. Pleasure began to coil again. Pressing his hands back, she began to ride him in earnest, drinking in his every sound of strain and pleasure, loving that she was doing this to him. Nothing had ever felt as good as having this man buried inside her, knowing he was hers and hers alone.

"Not gonna last much longer," he gasped.

"Then come."

"Not without you." He reached between them, finding her clit and sending her back into freefall with his name on her lips.

CHAPTER 8

Griff woke just after dawn. He'd barely slept at all, but four years of programming wasn't so easily broken, even after a night full of the best sex of his life. With his wife.

His wife.

Sam lay curled on her side, facing away from him. His arm tucked around her waist, his bigger body wrapped around her as the big spoon, ensuring his dick nestled against the curve of her ass. He considered stroking her to wakefulness, of sinking into her sweet body again as he had so many times last night. She was an addiction, and he'd wanted her again almost as soon as they'd caught their breath. Was it marriage? Love? Or was it simply her?

He'd never woken with a woman before, never felt the urge to start his day making love. Hell, he wasn't sure he'd ever made love before Samantha. No one had ever mattered like her before. No one had ever made him feel awed and protective and so very lucky.

Content, he pressed a soft kiss to her tattoo. She didn't stir at the touch, so he settled back against his pillow. She needed sleep, so he'd leave her be and try to get some more shuteye himself.

But his mind wouldn't turn off.

It was officially tomorrow. The practicalities that had seemed like distant mirages last night could no longer be ignored. She had a flight back to Raleigh this afternoon. Back to the real world life she was living, with grad school and grown-up aspirations. How exactly did he fit into that? They hadn't discussed any details of how a real marriage would work between them.

She'd be in school for several more years, and he… currently had nothing. No job, no prospects, no clue where to go from here. He could try college on his GI bill, but his grades in high school had never been stellar, even with her help, and he'd never felt like higher education was the right path for him. He had some money saved up, enough to last a while as he looked for some kind of employment. The idea of that hadn't bothered him when he'd planned this trip. But he hadn't had a wife then. Hadn't had anyone depending on him. Not that Sam was anything other than independent and capable of taking care of herself, but he wanted to be able to take care of her. Wanted to be someone she could rely on. Turn to. He wanted to be the man she'd promised that judge that he could be. She deserved nothing less. Hell, she expected nothing less. Her brother was a fucking SEAL. Nobody just fell into that. It was a calling. A duty. A grueling, tough-as-hell track that only the best of the best took.

Jesus.

He wasn't that guy. Not really. He'd done his duty in the Marines, but he hadn't pushed himself to be more. He'd counted down the days until the end of his service as if it had been the jail time he'd avoided. As if it was just something else to get through. There was nothing noble in that. Nothing meritorious that showed he'd done anything to be a truly better man.

How long would it take her to realize that she'd been wrong? How long until the strain of an unplanned marriage became too much? How long until she figured out he was a mistake, and she'd been blinded by old affection and lust?

Uncomfortable and needing space, he eased away, rolling out of bed to pace to the window. The sky was edging from gold to blue, on its way to being another beautiful day. But the sight brought him no peace. He was too busy thinking about the future and all the details they hadn't discussed. There'd be no more buffer of vacation or alcohol, nothing to soften the truth of who he really was.

He couldn't face disappointing her. Couldn't watch the change in how she saw him as reality replaced the fantasy she'd built up in her head. The shame of it bowed his shoulders.

Heart aching, he turned to look at Sam, memorizing the way her lashes fanned against her cheek, how her mouth curved into a gentle smile in sleep.

He'd been a fool to think they could do this. To believe they could have this. He'd done nothing to deserve someone like her. But he'd followed impulse, said yes, and kept saying yes even as he'd known deep down that he wasn't the man for her. Maybe a part of him had been hoping she'd be the one to put on the brakes, so he wouldn't have to do the hard thing. She'd always been the smart one. The sensible one. He just seemed to be her one true blind spot.

He could be selfish and try to keep her, hoping to outrun his bad decisions. Or he could do the right thing. Put in the work to become that guy she believed in. A man she could be proud of.

He'd just have to give her up to do it.

SAM WOKE IN STAGES, slowly surfacing as if coming up from an ocean dive. Exhaustion threatened to drag her back under, but the persistent gnawing in her empty belly was stronger. Consciousness brought with it awareness. Her body felt tender and used in the best possible way. She'd lost track of the number of orgasms. Just thinking about them had arousal stirring again. Griff would be okay if he'd turned her into a sex fiend, right?

She stretched and winced. Okay, maybe a soak first before the next round. They could wedge themselves into the tub together. Probably.

Intent on kissing him awake, she rolled over. But the bed was empty. Sam reached anyway, as if he were merely hiding under an invisibility cloak. But the sheets were cool.

She sat up, the covers pooling at her waist. "Griffin?"

He didn't answer.

Ears straining, she listened for movement in the bathroom. Nothing. A fact she confirmed a few moments later as she dragged herself out of bed.

He wasn't here.

Confused, and a bit headachy from lack of sleep and the champagne they'd polished off sometime in the night, she checked the clock. Two in the afternoon.

"Shit!" There wasn't a chance in hell she'd make her flight.

Okay. Okay, fine. They needed to make Griff's flight arrangements, too. She could reschedule. It was late, far later than she'd meant to be up. Maybe he'd gone in search of food. Her stomach growled at the thought as she began to search for a note.

He'd picked up. The clothes they'd shed on their return were no longer on the floor. Her dress was draped neatly over the desk chair. There was no sign of the suit. Maybe he'd popped out to return it? Probably smart. They'd missed check out already, so there'd be quite a few additional late fees tacked on to their weekend.

Maybe she should grab a shower and pack so she'd be ready to go when he got back. But she stopped in the bathroom, seeing only her toiletries on the counter.

Heart thudding, she moved back into the bedroom, switching on lights as she went. She spotted the tray from the strawberries, and the glasses beside the empty champagne bucket on the TV stand. Crushed rose petals still littered the floor and peeked out from the bedding, and a few of the electric candles still had enough charge to glow. But there was no sign of his duffel bag.

The last vestiges of sleep evaporated, replaced by a sick, thickening dread.

An envelope with her name scrawled across the front leaned against the mirror. Hand shaking, she picked it up, sliding out the contents. The top sheet of hotel stationery was a letter penned to her in his bold, masculine hand.

Dear Samantha,

These last days with you have been the best of my life. I want to emphasize that before I say what I need to say because I know you probably won't understand what comes next. Last night was beautiful. Special. Like you. I hope I was able to make you feel even a fraction of that. You are a gift I don't deserve.

A long time ago, you took a chance and made Judge Mosley a promise that I could be something better than I was. You believed in me, saw something no one else did. I didn't know that you were the reason I got a second chance. I don't know what would've changed if I'd known that back then, but it shames me to say that I didn't make the most of it. I'm not that guy you see in me. Not yet. But I'm going to keep that promise you made for me. I'm going to work to become that man because you deserve nothing less.

I re-upped with the Marines this morning. I

had just enough time to take care of a few things before I needed to fly out and report for duty. I know this will hurt you, and I'm sorrier than I can say that this is what you'll probably take away from our time together. I don't want to screw up any more of your life than I already have. Enclosed you will find divorce papers. Sign them and you'll be free of me. Free to live the amazing, fantastic life you were meant for. I don't expect you to wait for me. But someday, when I've truly kept that promise, become the kind of man you deserve, I'm coming back. And then we'll see.

Yours always,

Griffin

Tears dripped onto the page, and the ink began to run. Sam let the letter fall to the desk and glanced over the papers that followed. He'd already signed, throwing away their marriage after less than twenty-four hours. No discussion. No attempt to compromise or consider her thoughts or feelings.

He'd just decided they were through, without even talking to her.

Without even saying goodbye.

That felt like the worst betrayal of all.

She snatched up her phone, looking for a message, a missed call. Anything to indicate he'd changed his mind. But there was nothing. And she realized she couldn't even call him on his bullshit because he'd never given her his number.

She'd been ready to give this marriage a chance. To support him in whatever way he needed for the next phase of his life. She thought he'd been ready to do the same for her.

But that was a dream. A beautiful, foolish, lust-filled dream. One that was over.

I'm coming back.

It was an empty promise. Sam recognized that. A throwaway line probably meant to soften this blow. It did nothing but make her heart bleed more. She didn't dare believe he meant it because too much of her wanted to hope he'd realize he'd made a mistake and beg her for a chance to make things work.

But he wouldn't. He'd walked away. Left her to fend for herself.

And she needed to figure out how to go back to a life without him.

HOLD THE TOMATOES!

I KNOW. I *know!* This was so mean of me. I pride myself on not delivering cliffhangers because I hate them myself. But as I took great pains to try to communicate in the book description, the letter at the beginning, and on the cover, this story was a prequel novella. It is backstory and necessarily has an unhappy ending.

But the good news is that Griff *does* keep his promise. He does come back for her. And he'll have his work cut out for him in winning her back. *Come A Little Closer* is available now. Don't miss your chance to see these two come back together.

Turn the pages for a sneak peek at the opening chapter.

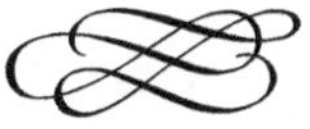

"Why did I agree to this wedding?" Samantha Ferguson demanded. "I hate weddings."

Audrey's voice on her car's speakers was dry. "I hope you don't since you agreed to be in mine."

She'd done so without a qualm, delighted that one of her best friends had found love with an amazing man. Watching the two of them fall for each other at a grown-up summer camp last year had been an absolute joy, even if it had given her a bit of a pinch around her own heart.

"You and Hudson aren't the same."

"And why is that?"

"For one, I'm not going to know the entire wedding party, and the entire wedding party is not going to have a whole boatload of stories about me that I'd rather forget. With Erin, there's this whole getting-the-band-back-together vibe. I haven't seen a lot of these people at all since high school and college, and we weren't exactly all buddy-buddy to begin with. It was one of those situations where she and I were friends, and I was tangentially associated with the rest of them."

How often that had been the case over the years. Her circles had always been small, which never bothered her until ceremony and celebration called for her to play nice with others. There was nothing like being thrust into a larger group to make her feel like an outsider.

"Is it really the whole idea of having to deal with people from high school that has you in a dither? You're not normally this agitated about the idea of going home."

Sam blew out a breath, unable to muster any annoyance at her friend putting on her therapist's hat. "I hated high school. You know that. It wasn't me. I didn't fit in, and I spent so much time and effort working to get myself away from all of that. I'm afraid that coming back for this wedding party bonding weekend crap that Erin has come up with is just gonna involve a whole lot of me getting forced back into roles that I don't want to remember." Just the idea of it had her shoulders bunching, her hands tightening on the steering wheel.

"Can they really force you back without your permission?"

On a scowl, Sam took the turn onto Main Street, automatically slowing as she rolled into what constituted downtown Eden's Ridge. "I think I liked it better when you weren't pursuing the shrinky side of your training, Dr. Graham. It's not so simple as permission. Obviously there's a conscious element to all this. But the bride and groom were a thing in high school, and I'm pretty sure they have much fonder memories of that experience than I did and are probably going to be playing up on that now that they found each other again. Oh, and then there's the fact that my high school nemesis is the matron of honor."

"You had a high school nemesis?" Audrey's tone piqued with interest, and Sam knew she was turning the idea of it over in her head. A certified prodigy, Audrey had graduated at fifteen, so she hadn't had most of the normal high school experiences.

"Cressida Gilcrest. Well, Milton now. She was a total Regina George. Except she never actually got her comeuppance and never became a better human. She's Erin's cousin, which is the only reason she's a part of this. Family pressure."

"Uh huh. And facing her down means what, exactly?"

"Having my always-a-bridesmaid status thrown in my face."

"What does that matter? You've never defined yourself by your relationship status."

Her back twitched, the tattoo on her shoulder seeming to burn. It and the memories it evoked were old, but the wound still throbbed. That was the real reason this weekend had her out of sorts. But she didn't confess that truth to Audrey. She'd never confessed it to anyone.

"You're right. Of course, you're right."

"I usually am."

"Har har."

Audrey laughed. "It's three days. You can handle it. There are worse things in the world than spending a long weekend at a spa."

"If this was all massages, facials, and pedicures, I'd be a lot less anxious about it." Seeing an open spot along the curb a block down from her mom's shop, Sam whipped into it.

"Well, put on your big girl panties because there's nothing to do about it but get through it. Didn't you tell me your bestie from high school was a bridesmaid, too?"

At the reminder, Sam's mind turned away from the hurt. "She is. Thank God. Jill's been in Atlanta for many years now, pursuing her career, and I've been on the publish or perish train, so it's been ages since we've actually connected. She's the lone silver lining of the weekend. We'll be able to bemoan our mutual single status together among all the marrieds."

"There you go. Focus on that and forget the rest."

"Right." The long exhale only released a little of the tension. She needed a change of subject before her too-observant friend started digging into more of the whys behind this anxiety. "In other news, how is my brother? I mean, I know you can't give me specifics because of the whole doctor-patient confidentiality thing, but generally how is he doing? He's been all incommunicado since he got up to Syracuse to start your program."

"He's good. He baked a chocolate tart this week that almost made me weep."

"I can't get over the fact that you're teaching my brother to be a baker." After more than a decade as a Navy SEAL, Jonah was finally out and working through his transition in Audrey's experimental treatment program.

"Well, let's be accurate. My future husband's cousin, Rachel, is the one who's doing the teaching. Overall, the program is performing well above my expectations. I mean, who would have thought that this would be an excellent treatment modality for PTSD, depression, and anxiety in a bunch of hard-core ex-military guys?"

"You did. And that's why you're the certified genius."

"Fair point. Now quit procrastinating and go get this over with. You'll feel better when it's done."

Busted. "Okay, okay, I know you're right, I'm gonna go. Do me a favor and tell Jonah to call home. I want to hear his voice and check in with him. Definitely mom will want the same."

"I'll let him know. Talk to you on the other side. I love you, girl, and I want you to remember I'm a professional, so hear me when I say this: You are a badass, intelligent, beautiful adult woman. Whatever shades of high school rear their ugly heads this weekend, you are not that person anymore, and nobody can make you be."

Though Audrey couldn't see, Sam smiled. "Yeah, I love you, too."

Hanging up the phone, she slid out of the car and into the cool October weather. Happy-faced pansies in concrete planters bobbed in the breeze as she made the short trek down the street to the salon known locally by all and sundry as the Snort 'n Curl, so dubbed because her mother, a former Miss Tennessee finalist, believed in big hair and big laughs. Her clients could count on both. That big, bawdy laugh rolled out the moment Sam tugged open the door, along with the chatter of cheerful female conversation.

The familiar scents of shampoo and the vaguely chemical undertone of hair dye and bleach drew her inside and back into her childhood. So much of her time growing up had been spent helping out in the shop, shampooing, sweeping up, doing homework. Snared in the past, she didn't immediately speak up. Here was comfort, camaraderie. Here was home, as much as the little three bedroom she'd once shared just a mile and a half up the road.

From beneath one of the bonnet dryers, Jolene Lowrey looked up. "Why, Samantha!"

Conversation came to a stop like the screech of a record.

Sam worked up a polite smile. "Mrs. Lowrey. Good to see you."

Rebecca set her comb and shears aside and rushed over, arms open wide. "Hey, baby girl!"

As those arms closed around her, another few layers of tension dropped away. "Hey, Mama." Sam burrowed in, briefly resting her head against her mother's shoulder as she wrestled with the guilt of not coming home as often as she should.

"It's so good to see you." Rebecca pulled back, looked her over with assessing eyes the same deep brown as Sam's. "You look a mite tired, honey."

Sam's lips twitched. "Good thing I'm here for a spa weekend, then."

"Girls' trip?"

She glanced over at the woman in the chair for a cut, recognizing Essie Vaughn, the dispatcher and admin for the Sheriff's Department. "Not exactly. I'm in town for a bachelor/bachelorette party bonding sort of deal for Erin Ashby and Kendrick Teague. Their wedding's coming up in a couple months, so they're getting everybody's together at The Misfit Inn and Spa for the weekend."

From the chair at the other station, Patty Hodgson tapped her lips. "Why do I remember his name?"

"He was star quarterback when I was in high school," Sam supplied.

"Oh yes, remember?" Essie prompted.

"He got scouted by UT. Went pro for a few years."

Rebecca returned to her station and resumed combing out and cutting Essie's hair. "Married some girl from out in California, I thought."

Essie nodded. "He did. She divorced him when he blew out his knee and lost his career."

"What about the Ashby girl?" Candice French continued to place rollers in Patty's hair. "I thought she married Galen Banks."

With an expression that was part pity part superiority that she wasn't as out of the loop as her stylist, Patty closed the magazine on her lap and crossed her legs. "She did. Moved off to Memphis, I think. They got divorced, too."

Amused at the play-by-play, Sam couldn't help clarifying. "Both of them came back to the Ridge to work at the high school. They reconnected and fell back in love. It's pretty adorable really. They were high school sweethearts." Even from her jaded perspective, she had to admit that. Love did come back around for some people.

"So lovely that they found their way back to each other." Essie sighed with the kind of contentment she'd often been known to display after finishing a good romance novel. Perking up, her eyes flicked to Sam's in the mirror. "What about you, dear? When are you going to walk down the aisle? Is there anybody special?"

The question was uttered in a cheerfully nosy tone that had Sam struggling not to grit her teeth. Because there wasn't anyone special. There hadn't been in more years than she cared to admit, and that trod far too close to the real reason weddings made her bitter. Because everyone pitied her for her perpetually single status, and no one knew she'd married and divorced at twenty-two. Then again, a marriage that lasted hardly longer than it took for the ink to dry didn't really count, did it?

Usually, she managed to shove that negativity down. But Kendrick had been close friends and foster brother to Griff, and she didn't want all those memories stirred back up. At least her ex-husband was still in the Marines, still off God knew where doing God knew what. She hoped he was safe, then cursed herself. Griffin Powell was no longer hers to worry about. He'd made his choice years ago, and it hadn't been her.

With no intention of sharing one of the most painful parts of her past, Sam forced another smile and focused on her mother. "I just spoke to Audrey on the way here. She said Jonah's doing well and promised to make sure he calls home."

Rebecca nodded in satisfaction. "Oh good. I've been sending care packages, but the boy hasn't done more than send a few emails since he got up there."

"Where is he these days?" Patty asked.

"Upstate New York in a program to help him transition from the SEALs to civilian life. He's training to be a master baker," Rebecca explained.

As conversation turned to the safer topic of her brother, Sam backed toward the door. "I need to be getting on. They're expecting me up at the inn. I just wanted to stop in and say hello."

"You're sure you won't stay at the house?" Rebecca asked.

"That would defeat the purpose of all of Erin's planned bonding activities. But I promise to stop by again before I head out. Love you, Mama."

"Love you, too, baby."

Check-in and farewells completed, she made a hasty exit, wishing the rest of the weekend would pass as quickly.

* * *

GRIFFIN POWELL WAS a man who understood duty. Twelve years in the Marines had seen to that. He made only those promises he believed he could keep, and he'd promised Kendrick he'd be here for this bizarre excuse for a bachelor party, even though he'd rather run fifteen miles uphill, with a hundred pounds of gear strapped to his back. Because Kendrick was his brother, and that's what brothers did. It wasn't Kendrick's fault that coming home felt so complicated or that weddings in general left Griff feeling edgy and restless.

No, that was entirely his own fault because of promises made and broken to a woman he'd never gotten out of his mind. A woman it was past time he sought out again. Griff was man enough to admit he was afraid of the reception he'd get. Afraid, too, of finding out she'd moved on with her life, as he'd freed her to do so many years ago. It had been the right thing for them both. He'd clung to that. Had to, or he'd never have been able to walk away. But that didn't mean he hadn't bled. Samantha had been his greatest love, and he wasn't ready to give up hope that he could still win her back.

Maybe he'd use this weekend to do a little digging. Find out where she was. If anyone knew whether she'd married. The idea tied his gut in knots. She and Erin had been friends once. Surely someone knew. With all the inevitable walking down memory lane, Sam would probably get mentioned without him having to say a word. He'd just have to bide his time and listen. He'd gotten good at that.

As he pulled up to the three-story Victorian that had been his home for the last three years of high school, Griff was grateful it wasn't his first trip back. The awkward had already been broached with his sisters earlier this year when he'd come as bodyguard to Kyle Keenan, and he hadn't been the prodigal in that scenario. Another foster brother, Kyle had become a rampant success as a country music star and finally come home to fix things with the woman who'd been his best friend. As Abbey was now his wife, and they were expecting their first child, that had all turned out all right in the end. Griff could only pray for such an outcome for himself.

Shaking off the somber mood, he dug up a smile and jogged up the steps, slipping in through the front door. It still felt right and comfortable to do that, though the home where he'd grown up had been turned into an inn. A part of him still expected his foster mother, Joan Reynolds, to come out of the kitchen, arms open wide for a hug. She'd been gone more than three years now, but he still felt the pang at her loss. At least until his sister, Kennedy, stepped out of the kitchen herself.

"Well, well. Look what the cat dragged in." Despite her tone, she was all smiles as she crossed the foyer, wrapping him in a warm hug of her own. "Welcome, home."

Griff squeezed her back. "Hey, sis. How are Xander and the baby?"

"He's protecting and serving and happy as a clam. The man was born to be sheriff. And Caroline is growing like a weed. She's started walking now and is into every blessed thing." Kennedy's grin communicated her absolute delight with her daughter. "How was the drive?"

"Eh, fine. No problems. Anybody here yet?"

"Oh yeah, everybody's been arriving all afternoon." She raised her voice. "Kendrick! Your brother's here."

The groom himself poked his head out of the living room that was now technically the guest lounge. A blinding white smile flashed in his dark face as he bulleted across the room, catching Griff around the middle in a move that was as much tackle as hug because they'd once been teammates as well as brothers. Griff set his stance, absorbed the momentum and hauled Kendrick into a rib-cracking hug himself. After a series of grunts and back thumps, they pulled back to beam at each other.

"Damn, it's good to see you, brother!" Kendrick's gaze swept the foyer. "Where's Mateo? I thought he was riding up with you from Nashville."

"Ah, well. He sends his regrets." Griff rocked back on his heels and shoved his hands into his back pockets. "He's not gonna be able to make it this weekend. His office manager recently quit, so there's nobody to manage the gym while he's away. But he promises he'll be here with bells on for the wedding."

"Damn. We'll miss him. But we're glad you made it." Erin Ashby, Kendrick's clearly besotted bride, crossed over to offer her own hug. "It's good to see you again."

"You, too." Out of long ago habit, he gave a gentle tug on Erin's blonde ponytail, making her laugh. "Who else is here?"

"Declan got in last night," Kendrick explained, mentioning yet another of their brothers. "Andy's working up at Thompson's Garage these days. He'll be along after work. And Erin's cousin, Ryder—you remember him? He married Lewis Washington a few years back. They run Forbidden Fruit Cidery now. He'll be by tonight with plenty of cider for the bonfire."

"About half my bridesmaids are here." Erin snuggled up against Kendrick's side. "Roxanne and Mariko."

"Did we hear our names?" A polished black woman in a neat pantsuit stepped out of the lounge, trailed by a petite Asian woman with laughing brown eyes and a waterfall of ebony hair.

"Ladies." Griff nodded in acknowledgement.

"And Cressida is here as well." Erin didn't quite manage to hide her speculative look. "She's in the spa at the moment."

Griff held in his wince. Barely. He hadn't seen his high school girlfriend in more years than he cared to count, and he wasn't eager to break the streak. She was just one of a long line of bad decisions from back then, none of which he wanted to remember.

Kendrick smirked. "She's married now."

"Thank God."

Erin's peal of laughter echoed in the foyer. "Good to know your taste has improved with age."

He offered a noncommittal grunt. He hadn't actually liked Cressida much when he'd dated her. She hadn't mattered, and that had been the whole point. She'd been convenient, and they'd used each other for their own ends. Not something he was proud of, but so little of his life back then could be looked at without cringing.

By his count, there were still a couple more bridesmaids unaccounted for. Griff realized he didn't have any idea who the rest of the bridal party was. He'd just agreed to be a groomsman for Kendrick without asking questions, trusting the rest would take care of itself. Before he could inquire about who else Erin had asked to stand up with her on her big day, the front door opened behind him. Griff turned in time to catch the bump of a rolling suitcase as the woman stepped into the room.

Everything inside him went still, and time seemed to slow and stretch as she straightened.

He wasn't prepared for this. Hadn't expected to see her. Not here. Not yet.

She was as beautiful as ever. Older, a little more polished, but she still bore the same faint smattering of freckles across her cheeks that looked like stars, still wore her mass of glossy brown hair long and loose. His fingers itched to reach out and touch her. To reacquaint himself with the silky feel of her hair, her skin. With the remembered taste of her mouth.

He'd taken half a step in her direction before she looked up, and he met those eyes that had haunted his dreams.

* * *

ORDER your copy of *Come A Little Closer* today!

OTHER BOOKS BY KAIT NOLAN

A complete and up-to-date list of all my books can be found at https://kaitnolan.com.

* * *

THE MISFIT INN SERIES
SMALL TOWN FAMILY ROMANCE

- *When You Got A Good Thing* (Kennedy and Xander)

- *Til There Was You* (Misty and Denver)
- *Those Sweet Words* (Pru and Flynn)
- *Stay A Little Longer* (Athena and Logan)
- *Bring It On Home* (Maggie and Porter)

RESCUE MY HEART SERIES
SMALL TOWN MILITARY ROMANCE

- *Baby It's Cold Outside* (Ivy and Harrison)
- *What I Like About You* (Laurel and Sebastian)
- *Bad Case of Loving You* (Paisley and Ty prequel)
- *Made For Loving You* (Paisley and Ty)

MEN OF THE MISFIT INN
SMALL TOWN SOUTHERN ROMANCE

- *Let It Be Me* (Emerson and Caleb)
- *Our Kind of Love* (Abbey and Kyle)
- *Don't You Wanna Stay* (Deanna and Wyatt)
- *Come A Little Closer* (Samantha and Griffin)

WISHFUL SERIES
SMALL TOWN SOUTHERN ROMANCE

- *Once Upon A Coffee* (Avery and Dillon)
- *To Get Me To You* (Cam and Norah)
- *Know Me Well* (Liam and Riley)
- *Be Careful, It's My Heart* (Brody and Tyler)
- *Just For This Moment* (Myles and Piper)
- *Wish I Might* (Reed and Cecily)
- *Turn My World Around* (Tucker and Corinne)
- *Dance Me A Dream* (Jace and Tara)

- *See You Again* (Trey and Sandy)
- *The Christmas Fountain* (Chad and Mary Alice)
- *You Were Meant For Me* (Mitch and Tess)
- *A Lot Like Christmas* (Ryan and Hannah)
- *Dancing Away With My Heart* (Zach and Lexi)

WISHING FOR A HERO SERIES (A WISHFUL SPINOFF SERIES)
SMALL TOWN ROMANTIC SUSPENSE

- *Make You Feel My Love* (Judd and Autumn)
- *Watch Over Me* (Nash and Rowan)
- *Can't Take My Eyes Off You* (Ethan and Miranda)
- *Burn For You* (Sean and Delaney)

MEET CUTE ROMANCE

SMALL TOWN SHORT ROMANCE

- *Once Upon A Snow Day*
- *Once Upon A New Year's Eve*
- *Once Upon An Heirloom*
- *Once Upon A Coffee*
- *Once Upon A Campfire*
- *Once Upon A Rescue*

SUMMER CAMP CONTEMPORARY ROMANCE

- *Once Upon A Campfire*
- *Second Chance Summer*

ABOUT KAIT

Kait is a Mississippi native, who often swears like a sailor, calls everyone sugar, honey, or darlin', and can wield a bless your heart like a saber or a Snuggie, depending on requirements.

You can find more information on this RITA ® Award-winning author and her books on her website http://kaitnolan.com.

Do you need more small town sass and spark? Sign up for <u>her newsletter</u> to hear about new releases, book deals, and exclusive content!

www.ingramcontent.com/pod-product-compliance
Lightning Source LLC
Chambersburg PA
CBHW070538100726
47907CB00004B/1175